THIS
LEAVENED
LAND

THIS LEAVENED LAND

A Novel of the Civil War in East Tennessee

THOMAS MAUSER

THIS LEAVENED LAND
A Novel of the Civil War in East Tennessee
by Thomas Mauser

First Edition
Copyright © 2025 by Thomas Mauser

Published by
Munn Avenue Press
300 Main Street, Ste 21
Madison, NJ 07940
MunnAvenuePress.com

Hardcover ISBN: 978-1-960299-87-1
Paperback ISBN: 978-1-960299-86-4

Printed in the United States of America

*To my Adriana,
my one true love, for everything.*

Contents

1

BEGINNINGS

"Never buy a mule for plowin' that ain't already broken to the plow...."

My father reminded me—a seventeen-year-old youth—of his homespun wisdom concerning mules as we took our horse and wagon from our farm to the village of Hunleyville in early April 1861 to buy a plowing mule. My father, William Meecham, a plain-spoken and God-fearing man, read the Bible every day and believed in the Old Testament proverb that a father who loved his sons chastised them often. Every time my two brothers, John and Charles, or I didn't behave the way our father wanted or didn't do our farm chores to his liking, he'd chastise us with his hickory switch.

Our fifty-acre farmstead lay some ten miles from Hunleyville. The village itself stood some miles north of Knoxville, Tennessee. It was in our simple farmhouse that my devout and strong-willed mother, Ellen Meecham, brought me into this world one cold winter afternoon—the eighth of December 1843 to be exact. I was given the Christian name James after my maternal Scots-Irish grandfather who settled in this part of Tennessee in the late 1700s. It was some years after my birth that my father and mother told me that they saw right quick after I was born that my left leg was a bit shorter than my right leg. I was thin and sickly as a child and walked with a limp, but farm work hardened me as I grew. Ninety years on, my left leg is still a bit shorter than my right leg and I still walk with a limp.

The rough-hewn country roads that my father and I traveled along in early April 1861 turned muddy when the rains came and were near impassable when the winter snows arrived. Hickory woodsmoke rose from the stone chimneys of scattered farmhouses as we drove past them. Farm fields hedged by worm fences lay ready for spring plowing and planting. We came to the near side of Hunleyville where a one-room schoolhouse and a square-shaped religious meetinghouse stood. Wooden-clapboard establishments stood along both sides of the rough country road that ran through the village—a cooperage, a clothing store, a general store, a gunsmith's shop, a doctor's office, a post office, and a boarding house. We passed a two-story courthouse with its barred cellar windows and high wooden gallows out back and soon came to the far side of the village where a grist mill, a blacksmith's shop, and a livery stable stood. Across from the grist mill stood a two-story, wooden-clapboard, dry goods store that was owned by my uncle, George Paynter. We halted in front of the store and climbed down from the wagon and walked into the store.

My cousins, David and Henry, were stocking the shelves, while my uncle was talking to one of our neighbors, a gray-haired and thickly mustached farmer by the name of Obadiah Adkins. After we said our hellos, Father and I listened as Obadiah told us that some of the local farmers were hankering to fight Yankees and others wanted to fight Confederates.

"It's all fools' talk," my father said.

"Why can't those politicians in Washington settle things?" my uncle asked.

"It's 'cause they can't agree on anythin'," Obadiah said. "That's why most folks reckon a war's comin'."

I knew not a lick about all the politicking that was going on in Washington at that time. *I ain't foolish enough to fight if a war starts*, I thought. Truth be told, I was a coward when it came to fighting in a war, and I knew that I'd skedaddle just as quickly as my legs could carry me once all the shooting started, and I told everyone so.

"Ain't nowhere a stays-at-home coward can hide once the fightin' starts, James," Obadiah said.

While my father and my uncle and Obadiah continued to talk, I spent some time with my cousins. David and I shared a strong liking for fishing and hunting, and we fell into talking about those pleasures. We were both seventeen years of age and shared the same birthday, but David always said that he was older than me because he was born in the morning and I was born in the afternoon. David, short in height and red-haired, was a high-spirited, stubborn, and foolhardy boy who often caused trouble for himself. I remember one hot summer day on our farmstead when I saw David throwing rocks at a wasp nest that was hanging on a tree near our farmhouse.

"Throwin' rocks at those wasps'll get you nuthin' but trouble, David," I said.

"Don't be tellin' me what I oughtn't to do," David said. "I knows what I'm doin'."

He kept throwing rocks at the nest until he knocked it to the ground. Sure enough, the wasps got plenty angry and chased him across one of our farm fields and into our barn. I hobbled toward the barn at a safe distance. When I got myself into the barn, I saw that David was trying to bury himself in a pile of hay that lay in a corner, but the wasps were stinging him plenty bad and he was hollering his head off.

My cousin Henry shared our liking for fishing and hunting, but he was more serious-minded than his brother and me. In this regard, he took very much after his father. Broad-shouldered, muscular, and of above-average height like his father, Henry was also older than David and me by four years and was the same age as my brother John and one year older than my brother Charles. My two brothers took mostly after Father and Mother. John was tall and strong like Father and always had a smile on his handsome face. Charles was also tall like Father and freckle-faced like Mother, and he had a roaring voice that could carry the length and breadth of a farm field. I, alas, took after neither Father nor Mother. Pale-skinned, blond-haired, average in height, and slightly narrow in chest, I had a rusty voice and was cursed with a somewhat shortened left leg.

After we bought our goods and said our goodbyes, Father and I walked over to the livery stable to buy our plowing mule. The stable was owned by a gray-haired, old free Negro man by the name of Absalom Johnson who lived and worked in Hunleyville. I had known and admired Absalom since I was a boy. He had been buying and selling horses and mules for as long as anyone could remember. Plenty of people came from all over the county to trade or buy a mule, a horse, or even a wagon from Absalom because he was always fair in his business dealings. Human nature being what it was back in those days (and still is today), there was always somebody who thought they could outsmart any Negro man, and they tried their darndest to take advantage of Absalom. He was a righteous man and always true to his word, but no one was ever able to put one over on Absalom because he was filled with godly wisdom when it came to the flimflam of men.

One of our neighbors liked to tell the story of his cousin, also a farmer, who came one day from another part of the county to Absalom's livery stable because he thought he could buy himself a good mule from that "old colored fool" (as he called Absalom) for next to nothing. Absalom got wise to him right from the start. They negotiated for a fair bit before they settled on a price, and the farmer paid Absalom for the mule. On the way back to his farm with his new mule, he paid a visit to his cousin and told him that he had gotten one over on that "old colored fool" and told his cousin how much he had paid for his mule.

"You damn fool, it's old Absalom who's gotten one over on you," his cousin told him. "You paid 'im more than anybody's ever done paid 'im for one of his mules."

That farmer who had tried to hornswoggle that "old colored fool" never got himself back again to Absalom and his livery stable.

In the same moment that my father and I said our helloes to Absalom that day in early April 1861, a young farmer pulled up with his mule and wagon.

"Who's the feller that owns this stable?" the farmer asked.

"You's lookin' at 'im," Absalom said.

The young farmer looked wide-eyed and slack-jawed at Absalom.

"You own this stable?" the farmer said, shaking his head. "Why hell, you ain't nuthin' but a goddamn n———r, and I sure as hell ain't buyin' nuthin' from no n———r," and he snapped his mule's reins and drove off.

The three of us stood and watched as the farmer drove his mule and wagon back down the country road that ran through Hunleyville.

"He oughtn't to have called you that, Mister Johnson," I said.

"I pays 'im no mind, James," Absalom said. "Most folks been

callin' me that since I was a boy. They reckon it's so I'll always knows my place, but I've gotten myself to payin' no mind."

The word "n——r" or the N-word was (and still is) a vile word. I have chosen not to write it out in these recollections of mine because it is a vile word. It was said plenty of times back in those days (and still is today) because most White people looked down on colored people. I never heard my father and mother say that word, and if my brothers or I ever chanced to say it, our father and his hickory switch chastised us right quick. Father and Mother oftentimes told me and my brothers that Absalom Johnson and people like him were decent people and they deserved to be treated decently.

We followed Absalom to the wooden stockades where he kept his horses and mules. While he was showing us his mule stock, we met another neighbor of ours, a fat, balding farmer by the name of Noah Boldt, who was also looking over Absalom's mules.

"You figure a war's comin', Will?" Noah asked.

"Got more important things to worry 'bout," Father said.

"Like buyin' himself a mule," Absalom said, and all of us chuckled except Noah.

"You've heard what that demon Lincoln's been sayin' 'bout us Southerners?" Noah asked.

"He's only wantin' to keep the country peaceable," Father said.

Noah glanced at Absalom.

"He's also tellin' us how we ought to treat this n——r and his kind," Noah said.

My father gave Noah a hard look and Noah caught my father's eye.

"I knows you like these colored folks," Noah said.

"They treat us fair and decent," Father said, "and we treat 'em the same."

"He ain't lyin' to you, Mister Boldt," Absalom said.

"I don't give a damn what a n——r has got to say 'bout anythin'," Noah said.

"I knows that, Mister Boldt," Absalom said. "But I'll still say what I knows needs sayin'."

Noah watched us like a coiled timber rattlesnake that was ready to strike as we looked over Absalom's mules. Father picked out a mule that he liked, gave it a good looking over, including its teeth, and, after asking Absalom if the mule was already broken to the plow and being told that it was, bought it from him. All the while, Noah and Father said no words to each other. Noah followed us as we took the mule, tied it to our wagon, and started for home.

"You Meechams ain't nuthin' but goddamned, African-worshippin' n——r lovers, and y'all can go to hell!" Noah hollered after us.

Everybody in our part of the county knew that Noah Boldt could turn the air blue around him or burn the ears off any mule or horse he was riding with his cussing. My family had been on friendly terms with Noah and his wife, Mrs. Emma Boldt, and their only son, Hiram, had been my friend. I first met Hiram when I was thirteen years old. My father had hired me out to help the Boldts with their spring plowing and planting. Hiram was gangly and had a mouth full of crooked teeth. While he plowed the farm fields with a single bottom plow and a mule, I planted the seeds by hand from a seed bag thrown over my shoulder. As we worked, we talked about good fishing spots, spooky backwoods forest trails, and the best places to hunt turkey and deer. Hiram showed me his Bowie knife and taught me how to throw it. I also learned from him that he was a couple of years older than me. As time passed, Hiram and I became friends.

One summer, Father and I helped Hiram and his father build a new worm fence in one of their farm fields. We tore apart the old fence, split the new rails from logs using hammers and wedges, and stacked them in a zig-zag pattern. Hiram and I—and our families— also met on Sundays at the religious meetinghouse in Hunleyville. Every fall Hiram and I hunted for turkey and deer with my brothers, or my cousins David and Henry, in a large forest called Stoneman's Wood near the Meecham farmstead. Every spring and summer Hiram and I went fishing for catfish in the nearby creeks.

One hot summer day when I was fourteen years old, Hiram and I took our wooden fishing poles and one of my father's mules and rode off to catch some catfish for dinner. We got to Mule Shoe Creek. It was wide and deep. Some old logs lay across the narrowest part of the creek so anyone could get across, but the logs were waterlogged and rotting. We got off the mule and started to walk across the logs. Hiram got over quickly, but I walked slowly on account of my left leg. Sure enough, I slipped and fell into the creek and was immediately overcome with fear because I didn't know how to swim. I tried to climb up the muddy creek bank, but I fell back because my wet clothes and soggy shoes began to pull me under the dark waters. I was starting to drown when I felt someone trying to pull me out. I looked up and saw Hiram was holding onto me. He began to pull me up when I slipped out of his hands and sank into the creek again. He pulled me up a second time, and this time he got me out. I was wet from head to toe, but I still had my fishing pole in my hand.

"You've saved my life!" I spluttered.

"I couldn't let a cripple like you drown," Hiram said, grinning.

I felt stung by that hurtful word, but I followed Hiram to the other side of the creek and we put our fishing poles into the water. Good fortune smiled on me for I soon caught a large catfish, and Hiram helped me to pull it out of the creek. We then crossed back, got back up on the mule, and made our way home. Father and Mother were standing on the front porch of our farmhouse when we arrived. They looked at me in my wet clothes and at the catfish hanging from my fishing pole.

"I reckon you went for a swim, James," my father said, "and a catfish caught you."

All of us laughed. After I told Father and Mother how Hiram had saved my life at the creek, they thanked him. We then ate the catfish for dinner. Before he left our homestead that evening for his family's farm, I asked Hiram a question.

"Why'd you call me a cripple back there at the creek?"

Hiram looked at me for what I took to be a long time.

"Well, ain't that what you is?" Hiram asked.

2

THE PECULIAR INSTITUTION

Like other farmers in our part of the county, every spring my father and my brothers and I plowed and planted our corn and wheat crops, and every fall we harvested our crops and sold them at the grist mill in Hunleyville. We also looked after our hens, roosters, and livestock, including cows and hogs. Mother cooked, sewed, washed, and helped us with the farm chores. Father also hired me and my brothers out to some of the local farmers to help with their spring plowing and planting so we could earn a little bit of extra money for our family. Father also hired me out from time to time to the only other free Negro man who lived and worked in Hunleyville, a tough and sturdy young cooper by the name of Jedediah Woodson.

Jedediah had come by mule and wagon to Hunleyville on a rain-swept afternoon in the fall of 1856. My father and I had come to my uncle's store that day to buy a few supplies for the farm and catch up on the village gossip. We were talking to Uncle George and his neighbor, Josiah McHenry, the pockmark-faced village grist mill owner, when a voice piped up behind us.

"I've been told that folks in these parts are lookin' for a cooper," the voice said.

We turned around. Standing before us was a young Negro man.

His worn jacket, pants, and shoes were wet and mud-splattered. A slouch hat sat tilted to one side on his head.

"Who's askin'?" my uncle asked.

"Name's Jedediah Woodson," the Negro man said.

The four of us introduced ourselves to him.

"Where're you from, Mister Woodson?" my father asked.

"From out near Nashville," Jedediah said.

"You've come a long ways lookin' for work," my father said.

"I reckon I have," Jedediah said.

"You learned your trade back in Nashville?" I asked.

Jedediah glanced at me and nodded.

"How'd a n——r get to be a cooper?" Josiah asked.

Jedediah gave Josiah a cold look and then proceeded to tell us that he was the son of a former slave whose dying owner had freed him and his kin on his deathbed some eight years before when Jedediah was nearly ten years of age. He had learned the cooper's trade, Jedediah said, from a free man of color who was a barrel maker in Nashville.

"We've already got one of your kind in this village," Josiah said.

"A cooper?" Jedediah asked.

"No," Josiah said. "A n——r."

My father gave Josiah a hard look but said nothing.

"We could use a cooper in this village," Uncle George said.

"You ain't got one?" Jedediah asked.

"We did a ways back," Father said, "but he got himself married to a girl over in the next county."

"You could stay with Absalom Johnson 'til you get settled," my uncle said. "He owns the livery stable across the road, and he's also...." He blushed.

"One of my kind," Jedediah said.

"If you're wantin' to," my father said, "I can take you over to Mister Johnson once we're done here, Mister Woodson."

"I'd be thankful to you," Jedediah said.

My father paid for the supplies we had purchased and he and I took Jedediah to the livery stable. After my father introduced him to Absalom, Jedediah went back to his wagon and mule and brought them to the livery stable. We helped him unpack his wagon and then my father and I went back to my uncle's store. While my father was untying our mule's reins, Josiah McHenry came out of the store and walked over to us.

"Will, you oughtn't to call that n——r Mister Woodson," Josiah said, "and that other n——r Mister Johnson."

Father and I climbed up into our wagon. Father grabbed hold of our mule's reins and looked at Josiah.

"I call 'em Mister Woodson and Mister Johnson 'cause I want to," Father said.

"Folks've been sayin' you Meechams treat that n——r Johnson better than you treat us White folks," Josiah said.

"Ain't ever cared much what anybody says 'bout us," Father said.

"You damn well better care, Will," Josiah said.

"Why?" Father asked.

"Folks'll turn their backs to you Meechams," Josiah said. "That's why."

"I reckon anybody who's doin' all this talkin' and turnin' is still doin' business with Mister Johnson," Father said.

"For heaven's sake, Will," Josiah said. "You know we've got to keep those people in their place. They ain't like us, and we oughtn't ever to treat 'em like they is."

My father shook his head.

"You're a damn fool, Josiah McHenry," Father said, and we headed back to our farmstead.

I learned early in my youth that most colored people in the state of Tennessee—men, women, and children—lived and worked and died as wretched slaves on White farms and plantations in the years before the Civil War. I met a colored slave for the first time in my life when I was eleven years of age and was hired out by my father as a field hand to a White farmer by the name of Roundtree.

It was the late spring of 1855 when my father and I went to the Roundtree homestead and met Mister Roundtree and his family at their ramshackle farmhouse. Roundtree was a large man. He shook hands with my father and then he looked at me.

"Your boy's standin' kind of crooked, Meecham," he said with a chuckle. "You're sure he's fit for workin' on my farm."

My cursed left leg always made me stand a bit crooked.

"I know my ways 'round a farm," I said.

"Is that so? Well, I reckon I'll find out soon enough if you's tellin' the truth," Roundtree said.

Out of the corner of my eye, I spied a strong young Negro man leaning against a near corner of the farmhouse. A shackle was wrapped around his left ankle, and the shackle had a trace chain to which was attached a small iron ball that he held in his hands.

"That's my wife," Roundtree said.

He jerked his thumb toward a woman who stood on the porch. She was short, as wide as a mule's backside, and as ugly as the devil.

"And that's my boy," Roundtree said.

He nodded toward a skinny young man who was sitting on the front porch steps. The young man looked at his father for a moment, and then he hugged his knees, shook his head, and laughed out loud.

"He ain't been right since the day he was born," Roundtree said. "My wife's been lookin' after 'im."

"Mister Roundtree, who's that feller lookin' at me?" I asked and pointed at the Negro man.

Roundtree looked back over his shoulder. The Negro man turned and walked away.

"That's my slave," Roundtree said. "His name's Lucas."

"You've got a slave?" my father asked.

Roundtree nodded.

"Bought 'im at a slave auction a ways back," he said. "I was needin' help with the chores. Some feller over in the next county owned 'im, but the feller had the consumption and couldn't keep Lucas no more."

My father and I glanced at each other.

"I've got to whip 'im plenty 'cause he's a lazy n——r," Roundtree said.

"Well, I reckon I'll leave my boy here for a spell to help you, Mister Roundtree," my father said.

"Suits me fine," Roundtree said. "There's plenty of work 'round here that needs doin'."

"We're needin' Mister Roundtree's money," my father whispered to me, "so do what he tells you to do, and don't do anythin' else. You understand?"

I nodded. I watched as Father climbed up into our wagon and left the Roundtree farmstead.

"There's lots of chores waitin' for you, boy," Roundtree said. "Ain't got no time to waste. You'll sleep in the lean-to back of the barn with Lucas, but don't you let 'im get you to bein' lazy."

I worked seven days a week for the rest of that warm spring and the long hot summer days that followed. Every day lasted from well before sunrise to well past sundown. Lucas woke me early every morning by hollering "Get up!" and told me to get to sleep every night by hollering "Shut your eyes!" I plowed farm fields, planted crops, hoed weeds, fed hogs and pigs and chickens, cleaned out the barn every day, milked cows, and did sundry other farm work. Sometimes Lucas and I did farm chores together. He was a close-mouthed man and carried his iron ball with him wherever he went. He worked hard and complained little, even when we toiled long hours together in the farm fields under the blazing summer sun.

From time to time, Roundtree cussed out Lucas or whipped him for no particular reason. One hot summer day, he started whipping Lucas because he had slowed down a bit while we were hoeing weeds. I screwed up my courage and spoke up.

"What you're doin' ain't right, Mister Roundtree," I said.

Roundtree stopped whipping Lucas and looked at me over his shoulder.

"He ain't ever done anythin' wrong," I said. "I know 'cause I've been watchin' 'im while he's been workin'."

A mean look spread across Roundtree's wide, ugly face.

"And you ain't got no reason to call 'im a n——r," I said.

In the next instant, Roundtree turned and kicked me hard, and I fell to the ground.

"I own 'im!" he hollered. "And I'll treat 'im any ways I like, and I'll call 'im anythin' I want! And there ain't nobody in this here god-damn county who'll tell me different!"

All the while, Lucas said nothing. After that day's farm chores were done and evening had settled over the sun-baked land, I limped behind Lucas as we made our way to the lean-to. Inside, the smell of human sweat hung thick in the warm, stale air. A single-lit candle provided the only source of light. After we sat down, Lucas leaned close to me.

"I reckon that Roundtree feller's standin' outside right now just so's he can hear what we's talkin' 'bout," he whispered.

He grabbed the trace chain and shook it.

"I've got to kill 'im so's I can get myself free," Lucas said. "And you're goin' to help me kill 'im."

I stared at him.

"I ain't wantin' to kill Mister Roundtree," I said.

"Why ain't you?" Lucas asked. "You said all those words to 'im 'bout me this mornin'. Was you lyin' to 'im?"

"I wasn't lyin' to 'im," I said.

Lucas grabbed my arm.

"If you wasn't lyin'," he said, "then you's goin' to help me kill 'im. Like I done said, there ain't no ways I can get free without killin' 'im."

He grabbed the trace chain again and shook it.

"Mister Roundtree's got a family," I said. "Don't you care 'bout 'em?"

"They don't mean nuthin' to me," Lucas said.

He let go of my arm and leaned back against the wall of the lean-to.

"If you kill 'im," I said, "they'll sure as heck catch you. And when they catch you, they'll hang you."

Lucas looked away. For a moment or two silence fell like a heavy curtain between us.

"You got any kin, Lucas?" I finally asked.

Lucas shook his head.

"My ma died a long ways back."

"And your pa?"

"Ain't ever knowed 'im. My ma done told me he was sold off to a White farmer the day I was born."

"You ain't got no other kin?"

Lucas shook his head again.

"I've got kin," I said, "and I miss 'em plenty."

"The Almighty's blessed you, boy."

"I know."

"I've suffered like Job in the Old Testament since the day I was born."

"Maybe we could be kin while we're workin' together."

Lucas looked at me.

"If we's kin, then you's goin' to help me kill 'im," he said.

I shook my head.

"I ain't goin' to help you kill 'im," I said.

Lucas leaned close to me, grabbed my arm, and squeezed it hard.

"Then you and me ain't no kin," he said. "And don't you get any idea in your head 'bout tellin' anybody that I'm wantin' to kill that Roundtree feller."

"I ain't goin' to tell," I said.

He squeezed my arm harder.

"If you does," he said, "I swear to God Almighty I'll kill you."

He roughly let go of my arm and laid himself down on his blanket.

"Shut your eyes!" Lucas shouted, and he soon fell asleep.

Summer passed and one day my father came back to the Roundtree farmstead with our wagon and mule. I said goodbye to

Mister Roundtree, trudged over to our wagon, and climbed up next to my father. I looked around and saw Lucas leaning against the farmhouse holding the iron ball in his hands. He stared at me for a time and then he spat on the ground and walked away. In the next moment, Mister Roundtree walked up to our wagon.

"My boy give you any trouble, Mister Roundtree?" my father asked.

"He done his work like I told 'im," Roundtree said. "But you'd better set 'im straight 'bout my n———r."

My father glanced at me. Roundtree tossed a small pouch up to my father.

"That's the money the boy earned for doin' his chores," he said.

My father and I headed back to our farmstead. That night, after Father had counted out the small pile of silver coins I had earned by the sweat of my brow, he sat me down.

"What did Mister Roundtree mean by sayin' I ought to set you straight 'bout his slave?" my father asked.

I told him about Lucas, how Mister Roundtree treated him, and what I said to Mister Roundtree that day when he whipped Lucas. And then I remembered my promise to Lucas and I didn't tell my father about Lucas's wicked scheme.

"He's Mister Roundtree's property," Father said. "He ain't ours."

"He wants to be free."

"I know he does."

"But it ain't right he ain't free."

"I know it ain't right. But it's the way things is. Been that way for a long time."

"Is every slave wantin' to be free?"

"Yes."

"How're they goin' to get free?"

"The Good Lord'll help 'em."

"When?"

"In His own time."

"How?"

"In His own way."

My father never hired me out to the Roundtree farm again.

3

Charlotte

The Meecham family—and most everyone else—was full of religion back in those days. Every Sunday was a day of rest because the Good Book said that Almighty God created Heaven and Earth in six days and He rested on the seventh day. Every Sunday morning Mother read to us from the Bible before we went to Reverend Gideon Trumbull's meetinghouse in Hunleyville to listen to his sermons and join the rest of the congregation in singing hymns and praying. Father's stout cousin, Robert Burden, his short, plump wife, Sarah, and their skinny young sons, Franklin and Billy, also came to the meetinghouse. Aunt Elizabeth (my mother's sister), Uncle George, and my cousins Henry and David also came every Sunday. After all the preaching, singing, and praying was done, the Burdens and the Paynters would come to our farm for lunch, and sometimes my cousins, my brothers, and I would run around the barn to see who would win. Sure enough, my brother John won every time because he was the fastest, and I was always last because of my somewhat shorter left leg.

It was also to the reverend's meetinghouse that Judge Samuel Benjamin Endicott and his wife, Mrs. Abigail Endicott, came every Sunday with their daughter, Charlotte. I first met Charlotte in the late summer of 1860 when I was sixteen years of age and attended the one-room schoolhouse in Hunleyville for the first (and only) time in my life. Most of the local farmers' sons and daughters in our part of the county got their schooling done toward the end of each summer after the planting and weeding seasons were done and before the fall harvest began. I learned a bit of reading and writing and arithmetic in school that summer, but I also played hooky once or twice and went fishing instead of learning the three R's. On my first day of school, I saw a pretty young girl standing outside the schoolhouse talking to a man and a woman whom I took to be her father and mother. I screwed up my courage and slowly walked up to her.

"Hello," I said. "This is my first day in school. Is this your first day, too?"

The young girl glanced at me.

"Yes, it is," she said.

"My name's James Meecham," I said.

She glanced at me again.

"That's nice," she said.

"I haven't seen you before," I said.

She turned and looked squarely at me.

"We have just moved here," she said. "My father—" She glanced at the man. "Is Judge Samuel Benjamin Endicott, and he is the new judge in Hunleyville, and my mother, Mrs. Abigail—"

"Charlotte," her father said, "this poor, ignorant, farm boy does not need to know our family business."

He gave me a cold stern look. He wore a goatee and was well-dressed. Charlotte and her mother were likewise well-dressed.

"But, Father, you were once a poor, ignorant, farm boy," Charlotte said.

Her father turned his cold stern gaze from me to Charlotte.

"That was a long time ago," he said.

"Mister Abraham Lincoln of Illinois was also once a poor, ignorant, farm boy," Charlotte said.

"Never mention that man's name in my presence," he said. "He is the devil incarnate."

"Please, for goodness' sake, could we talk about something else?" Charlotte's plain-faced and slightly cross-eyed mother inquired.

She sighed, then looked me up and down.

"I see this school teaches poor, ignorant, crippled, farm boys," she said.

That damned left leg of mine again. I blushed, and a sharp rush of anger and shame rose up within me. The schoolhouse bell rang. Charlotte said her goodbyes to her mother and father and followed the other boys and girls into the schoolhouse. I turned away from Charlotte's parents and followed her into the school.

I never sat near Charlotte in the classroom while the teacher taught the class the three R's. From time to time I stole a glance in Charlotte's direction and hoped—and prayed—that she would catch my eye. Sometimes I saw her writing on her slate board or in her notebook or reading her school primer, like the rest of us. Other times I saw her exchange glances or smiles with one or another of the schoolboys who were lucky enough to sit near her, and I was overcome with jealousy. I was forever looking at Charlotte's pretty face—her large brown eyes framed by long brown curls and her beautiful smile—and my stirrings of love for her burned brighter and deeper every time I gazed at her.

During those times when Charlotte caught my eye in the schoolyard during our class breaks, I immediately tried to show off by challenging an older schoolboy to a wrestling match to win her undying admiration. I had oftentimes wrestled with my older brothers on our farm, and that hard-earned experience now stood me in good stead in the schoolyard. But, alas, it did not help me win Charlotte's attention. However, one day late that summer while I was talking to a schoolboy during a class break about fishing and hunting, I caught her eye.

"I'll bet you I can walk on my hands," I blurted out to him.

The schoolboy stared wide-eyed at me for a moment, and then he shook his head.

"I'll bet you can't," he said.

I got myself up on my hands and slowly "walked" about the schoolyard. I was feeling rather proud of myself when another schoolboy walked up to me and pushed me over. I fell to the ground and lay there while the two schoolboys stood over me and laughed at me.

"It don't matter which way you walk, Meecham," the schoolboy who had pushed me said. "You'll always walk crooked 'cause you's a cripple."

The two schoolboys laughed again and walked away. I got up from the ground, dusted myself off, and looked about for Charlotte. I spied her on the other side of the schoolyard. Her back was turned to me and she was talking to a small knot of schoolgirls. Filled with embarrassment, I made my way past the various knots of boys and girls in the schoolyard, walked into the empty classroom, sat down at my desk, and buried my face in my hands. *I'm such a darn fool*, I thought. The schoolhouse bell rang to call everyone to class, and at that moment in my young life, I resolved never to like Charlotte again.

My school days came to an end on the last day of summer in 1860. Fall came and with it, the yearly harvest season began. After we had gathered our wheat and corn crops, I traveled by wagon and mule to Hunleyville a number of times to deliver the Meecham harvest to the village's grist mill. During one of my trips, I saw Charlotte and her mother, but I paid them no mind.

When the harvest season came to an end, Reverend Trumbull held a special prayer service in the village meetinghouse to give thanks to the Almighty for a bountiful harvest. The reverend—everyone called him the "Old Preacher" because he was gray-headed and had a long gray beard—stood before us and led us in a prayer of thanksgiving. While we were praying, I spied out of the corner of my eye Charlotte and her parents sitting a little ways away from me and my family. I looked in her direction and caught her eye. She smiled at me and turned back to her praying. After the reverend spoke his final blessings, scattered cries of "Praise the Lord!" and "Hallelujah!" filled the air. With the prayer service concluded, everyone made their way out of the meeting house.

"James!" a familiar voice called out.

Charlotte walked up to me with her parents following close behind. As quickly as her parents saw me they turned and made their way out of the meetinghouse.

"It's nice to see you again, James," Charlotte said.

"It's nice to see you, Charlotte," I said, and I blushed.

Her pretty face and her large brown eyes were still framed by long brown curls and her smile was still lovely. My late summer resolution about her began to weaken.

"I saw you in the village a while back," she said, "but I guess you didn't see me."

"No, I didn't," I lied, and I blushed again.

"That's all right," she said. "What have you been doing since we finished school?"

She listened with what I took to be interest to my tales of daily farm chores, fishing, and hunting wild turkey and deer in Stoneman's Wood.

"Hunting deer and turkey? That sounds adventurous!" she exclaimed.

"Yes, I reckon it is," I said. "What've you been doing?"

She told me about the poems and the romance novel that she had been reading since the end of school. I was not a bookworm, but I listened with interest as she talked about her favorite poet, Elizabeth Barrett Browning, and her favorite novel, *Jane Eyre,* by Charlotte Brontë.

"Charlotte!" a voice called out.

We looked in the direction from where the sound of the voice came from and saw Charlotte's father standing in the doorway of the religious meetinghouse.

"I have to go, James," she said. "It's been really nice talking to you."

She hesitated for a moment. "Maybe we could meet after Sunday services and talk about things like your hunting adventures and my Elizabeth Browning poems?" she asked.

"Yes, I'd like that a lot," I said, and I blushed a third time.

My late summer resolution about Charlotte crumbled to dust. Charlotte and I met every Sunday after the reverend's service. We walked up and down the village, peered through store windows, and talked about poetry, *Jane Eyre,* fishing, hunting, and farm life. Charlotte recited whole stanzas of Elizabeth Browning's poetry, while I told her how I caught catfish and how I tracked and shot wild turkey and deer. After each of our Sunday walks, I escorted Charlotte back to her family's large red brick house on the outskirts of the village.

One Sunday afternoon, I took Charlotte to the livery stable where I introduced her to Absalom Johnson and the three of us spent some time looking at Absalom's stable of horses. As the days and weeks passed, my love for Charlotte grew more passionate and I left little heartfelt notes of affection for her at the village post office. To my great joy, she reciprocated with small notes of affection for me.

My mother and father knew that I spent time with Charlotte, but they did not say a word about the matter. My brothers, on the other hand, teased me without end. After each Sunday service, John and Charles would shout into my ear, "Jimmy loves Charlotte! Jimmy loves Charlotte!" before they and my parents made their way home by mule and wagon. I remained behind with one of our mares to ride home after my weekly outing with Charlotte.

As fall turned to winter, I told my father and mother that I wanted to give Charlotte a gift for Christmas. My father gave me a few coins from the money I had earned from the recent summer's farmwork that I had been hired out to do.

"I hope you ain't barkin' up the wrong tree," he said.

"I ain't," I said.

I went to the general store in Hunleyville, found the item that I was looking for, and went up to the counter to pay for it. The young store clerk looked at the book and then he looked at me.

"Ain't ever seen you buy a book," he said.

"Always wanted one of 'em."

"You know how to read?"

"I get by."

"Didn't think you had any schoolin'."

"Got some."

"I got some, too, but I still don't know how to read."

I paid for the book and walked out of the store with a collection of Elizabeth Barrett Browning's poetry under my arm. That Sunday before Christmas Day, my family and I went to the reverend's meetinghouse as usual. I saw Charlotte with her father and mother. I slowly walked up to her, wished her a merry Christmas, and gave her my gift.

"Come with us this instant, Charlotte," her slightly cross-eyed mother snapped.

"Yes, Mother dear," Charlotte said.

She gazed at the book and leafed through its pages, and all the while her parents glared at her. Her mother sighed and she and Charlotte's father turned and walked into the religious meetinghouse.

"Thank you for this beautiful gift, James," she said. "I will always treasure it."

She brought her pretty face up close to my face. "And I will always treasure you," she said.

In that magical moment, the deep love that I felt so passionately in my heart for Charlotte overwhelmed me.

"And I'll treasure you forever, Charlotte," I said, and I kissed her.

"Jimmy loves Charlotte! Jimmy loves Charlotte!" my brothers shouted.

Charlotte glanced over her shoulder at my brothers and laughed, while I, frozen with embarrassment, blushed.

4

REBELLION

It was the middle of April 1861 when my father's cousin, Robert Burden, rode up with his mule and wagon at a furious pace to our farmstead as we were planting our annual crops. He breathlessly told us the news that Confederate forces in South Carolina—the first Southern state to leave the Union in December 1860—had fired upon and seized Fort Sumter, a federal citadel in Charleston, South Carolina.

"What does that mean?" I asked.

"It means a fearsome storm's comin' over this land," Robert said. "It means war!"

My father and my brothers and I looked at each other. My father told his cousin he was worried about his farm.

"If they square off on my land," Father said, "and get to fightin' each other, I ain't sure what I'll do."

I sure ain't goin' to fight in this war, I thought.

A couple of days later, my brothers went to Hunleyville to buy more corn seeds. After they returned, they told us that the only news people were talking about was the fall of Fort Sumter and President Lincoln's request for 75,000 volunteers to fight the Confederacy. My brothers also told us that Noah Boldt was shouting for everybody to hear that anyone who stood with Lincoln ought to be hanged or shot, and if no patriotic Confederate in this part of the county was willing to do the hanging or shooting, then, by God, he'd do the hanging and shooting himself.

"Noah Boldt's just talkin' nonsense," Father said, "like he's always doin'."

"Maybe," Charles said. "But there's plenty of folks who've said they agree with 'im."

My brothers looked at each other for a moment.

"You've got somethin' else that needs sayin'?" Father asked.

My brothers looked at their shoes.

"Spit it out," Father said.

"Well, me and Charles... we've decided to fight for Lincoln," John said.

Mother let out a groan and shook her head. I reckoned my brothers' friends must have told them they were joining Lincoln's army and my woodenheaded brothers foolishly decided to follow them.

"Just 'cause you're wantin' to fight," Mother said, "don't mean you've got to."

"We've got to save the Union," Charles said.

"What about our farm?" Father asked. "Ain't it worth savin'?"

"I know it's our farm," John said, "but the Union's worth more to me and Charles."

"I sure hope you boys know what you're gettin' into," Father said.

"We'll stay till the fall harvest's brought in," Charles said.

"James can still help you with the farm chores after we've left," John said.

"I ain't helpin' with the farm chores," I said.

"What d'you say?" Father asked.

" I ain't stayin' here no more," I said.

"Why not?" Mother asked.

"Are you wantin' to join Lincoln's volunteers?" Father asked.

"No, I ain't wantin' to join no volunteers," I said.

"Stop all this fool-headed talkin', Jimmy," Mother said.

"It ain't fool-headed talkin'," I said.

"Get to your farm chores, James," Father said.

Filled with resentment and anger, I trudged off toward the barn. *My stupid brothers have ruined everything*, I thought. I was a dutiful son, but I had lately come to hate farming. My dream had been to work with horses. I once told Absalom Johnson—in secret—about my dream and he had promised me a job at his livery stable. Now, with my brothers marching off to war, my dream of working with horses was gone.

My love of horses began at the age of twelve when I was given the daily chore by my father of looking after our two mares and our stallion. I soon wanted to learn how to ride a horse like my brothers. One day, I asked my father if he could teach me.

"You ain't got grit," Father said. "They'll buck you off just as quick as you get up on 'em."

His harsh words cut me to the quick. However, after some time had passed, a firmness of mind settled upon me. *I've got plenty of grit*, I thought, and I kept after my father every chance I had. After several months of caterwauling about wanting to ride a horse, my father gave way.

"You've plumb worn me out," he said. "But if you break a bone doin' it, you ain't ever goin' to ride 'em again."

I saddled and bridled one of our mares, led her out onto one of our farm fields, got myself into the saddle, kicked her flanks, and shouted "Go!" Sure enough, she bucked. I flew out of the saddle and landed hard on my backside. I tried again and landed on my backside a second time. On my third try, the mare bolted across the farm field while I hung on for dear life. I finally pulled up on the reins, brought her to a halt, and steered her back to our barn where Father stood waiting for me.

"Well, I reckon you've got grit, James," Father said, and a rare smile creased his weathered face.

A couple of days after we learned that my brothers were enlisting in Lincoln's army, my father sent me to help our neighbor Obadiah Adkins with his farm chores, and it was there that I chanced to meet Noah and Hiram Boldt.

"What're you doin' here, Meecham?" Hiram asked with a smile, revealing his crooked teeth.

"I'm here to help Mister Adkins with his chores," I said.

"You're standin' on Confederate land," Noah said.

"If you stand for Lincoln, Meecham," Hiram said, "you ain't welcome here."

"Is that true, Mister Adkins?" I asked.

Obadiah's thick mustache twitched, but he said nothing.

"You Meechams stand for Lincoln, don't you?" Noah asked.

"Lincoln's our president," I said. "That's what my pa told me."

"Those Yankee slavery haters," Hiram said, "are wantin' to free all the colored folks down here in the South."

"And they're wantin' to take our land," Noah said, "so's they can give it to all them colored folks."

"We know Lincoln's a Yankee slavery hater," Hiram said.

"Are you a Yankee slavery hater, Meecham?" Noah asked.

"He told us Lincoln's their president," Obadiah said, his thick mustache twitching.

"Then you're against us, Meecham," Noah said.

"Why, hell, if this cripple's against us," Hiram said, "this war'll be over lickety-split." They all laughed at me.

"You'd best get off my land, Meecham," Obadiah said, his thick mustache twitching again, "and don't ever think of comin' back."

I journeyed home from the Adkins farmstead filled with a burning resentment towards Noah Boldt and Obadiah Adkins and a smoldering hatred of my one-time friend, Hiram Boldt.

In the spring days that followed the surrender of Fort Sumter, some of the local farm boys were eager to enlist in the Confederate army. One morning in late May, the oldest of our nearby neighbor Samuel Tyrrell's three sons, Philip, came to our farm and told us that he was wanting to go to North Carolina to join one of the Confederate army regiments that was forming up in that state. Philip was a thin, bucktoothed, and God-fearing farm boy, and he had oftentimes gone fishing with my brothers. He asked my brothers if they wanted to come with him to join the Confederate army.

"They're joinin' Lincoln's army," Father said.

"Is that the truth, John?" Philip asked.

John looked squarely at Philip.

"It's true," John said.

Philip gave each of us a hard look.

"If I ever square off against any of you Meechams," he muttered, "I'll send you to hell," and he left our farm.

We kept to our farm chores that spring and attended Reverend Trumbull's Sunday preachings as always, but the warmer days brought me much heartsickness and melancholy about Charlotte.

Her father and mother still came every Sunday to the meetinghouse, but Charlotte was nowhere to be seen. Truth be told, I had not seen her since the first thaw in mid-March. My handwritten notes of affection to her still remained at the village post office.

On the last Sunday of May 1861, we listened to Reverend Trumbull preach about the Old Testament story of the brothers Cain and Abel. The "Old Preacher" told us how God put the mark of His curse on Cain after he had slain his brother Abel and condemned him to wander the length and breadth of the land. The reverend then pointed his long, bony forefinger at us.

"As it happened to Cain, so it'll be by God's right hand to anyone who raises a hand against the Confederacy!" he cried out.

After the service ended, a large crowd gathered outside the meetinghouse and shouted their support for the Confederate States.

"I'm goin' to hang Lincoln!" Noah Boldt hollered, and the crowd cheered.

In that moment of high emotion, I saw Charlotte among the crowd and my heart leaped into my throat. She was standing at the edge of the crowd and was holding onto the arm of a well-dressed man who stood beside her. My heart, until that moment full of an aching love for her, broke. I turned away from the still cheering crowd. Downcast, I shambled toward our family's wagon. I had just put my hand on one of the wagon wheels when I heard Charlotte's voice call out my name, and I turned around. Charlotte walked up to me while still holding onto the arm of the well-dressed man.

"Hello, James," Charlotte said. "I want you to meet Mister Matthew Pelham."

Matthew and I exchanged hellos.

"Matthew and I have known each other for some time," she said.

"For quite some time, my dear Charlotte," Matthew Pelham said. "We have known each other since we were quite young."

An overwhelming heaviness filled my heart.

"Matthew and I have reached an understanding," Charlotte said, "and his family seems well pleased."

They looked at each other and smiled.

"James and his family are farmers, Matthew," Charlotte said.

"I am certain that it is a life that is most pleasant to them," Matthew said.

"Yes, I am sure it is," Charlotte said. "Well, goodbye, James. I will always fondly remember you as agreeable company for me."

"Goodbye, Charlotte," I said.

A great depression of spirits settled over me as we journeyed home. My brothers stole sideways glances at me from time to time, but they said nothing. The only sounds to be heard during the entire ride home were the jolting and creaking of our wagon, the jingling of our horses' bridles, and the plodding of their hoofs on the rough country roads.

On the eighth day of June 1861, most Tennesseans—except a majority of those who lived in eastern Tennessee—voted to leave the Union and join the Confederacy. Before the votes were cast (only men could vote at that time), public gatherings were held in our part of the county, where speeches by Judge Endicott urged the citizenry to vote for secession. A couple of days after the vote was held, my brothers and I went to Hunleyville to buy goods at our uncle's store. As we left the store, we saw a crowd in front of the courthouse and Judge Endicott was standing on the courthouse steps. We walked over to the gathering and stood at the back of the crowd.

"Tennessee has found its courage!" Judge Endicott shouted.

The crowd cheered. Men tossed their hats in the air and women waved their handkerchiefs.

"God bless the Confederacy!" someone cried out.

The crowd kept cheering as my brothers and I made our way to our wagon and went home. *A fearsome storm is coming across this land*, I thought.

5

Vigilance Committee

Nearly two months after Tennessee joined the Confederacy, an eastern Tennessee Union newspaper reported the news that a Union army force was defeated by the Confederate army in the first major battle of the war. The two armies had met on July 21 at Bull Run Creek near Manassas Junction in northern Virginia. The Confederate army forced the Union army—along with scores of Union civilians and northern politicians who were spectators at the battle—to beat a hasty retreat back to Washington, DC. Confederate citizens in Hunleyville and the surrounding rural areas called it a "great victory," while those of us who stood for Lincoln and the Union were silent.

Soon after the battle at Bull Run Creek, printed declarations appeared in the village of Hunleyville and on rural crossroads posts in our part of the county.

A Proclamation
Hunleyville Vigilance Committee

Men of East Tennessee!

Rally to the aid of your oppressed Country!
Come to the Hunleyville Courthouse and join Hiram Boldt's
mounted Confederate Partisans to drive the foe from our land.

Signed,
Judge Samuel Benjamin Endicott, Esq.,
Committee Chair
Samuel Tyrrell, Committee Member
Noah Boldt, Committee Member

The annual harvest began that fall of 1861, and I soon took the first of our harvested crops to the grist mill in Hunleyville. The mill's owner, Josiah McHenry, told me that Hunleyville's Vigilance Committee had given him the names of local farmers who supported Lincoln and had told him in no uncertain terms that he was to have no further dealings with them.

"Your family's on the blacklist," Josiah said. "I ain't buyin' your crops no more."

A grin spread across his pockmarked face.

"I don't believe you, Mister McHenry," I said.

"It's God's honest truth," he said.

A cold spasm of fear overcame me in that moment.

"But it's harvest time, Mister McHenry," I said. "Where'll we find another grist mill that'll take our crops?"

"Don't know," he said.

"What do I do now?" I asked.

"Get over to the courthouse," Josiah said, "and swear an oath of allegiance to the Confederacy."

"Ain't no chance in hell that's goin' to happen," I said.

"Then you ain't got no chance in hell of sellin' your crops anywhere in this county," Josiah said.

"Has anyone said anythin' against this blacklist?" I asked.

"Heard tell that Absalom Johnson and Jedediah Woodson said some words," Josiah said.

"What happened to 'em?" I asked.

A smile creased Josiah McHenry's face.

"Vigilance Committee ran 'em out of here night before last," he said.

Josiah told me that Noah Boldt had taken over Absalom Johnson's livery stable and another of our neighbors, Sam Tyrrell, had gotten his nephew to take over Jedediah Woodson's barrel-making business. I hurried over to my uncle's store. The only people I found inside were my uncle and my two cousins.

"You've heard what happened?" David asked.

"Mister McHenry told me," I said.

Uncle George told me that ruffians had come to the store the previous night and warned him that he and his family would be run out of the village if they didn't swear an oath to the Confederacy.

"Who was leadin' 'em?" I asked.

"Hiram Boldt," my uncle said.

I felt a sharp sliver of anger pierce my heart.

"Emmett and Otis Tyrrell were with 'im," Henry said.

Sam Tyrrell's two younger sons each had the reputation of a

deadly timber rattlesnake—you crossed them at your peril.

"All three of 'em had guns," David said.

"We told 'em we weren't takin' the oath," my uncle said.

"I'll fight 'em all till kingdom come!" David shouted.

"You're not goin' to do any fightin'," my uncle said.

David remained silent, but I knew his rash words and brash temperament would sooner or later get the better of him. My uncle told me that he and his sons would help any farmers in the area who were for Lincoln by bringing them supplies from time to time in the dead of night.

"What if they catch you?" I asked.

"They won't," Uncle George said.

I was filled with doubts about my uncle's sense of confidence as I walked out of his store and I took my crops—and my fear—back to my family's farmstead.

Father and I traveled mile upon mile by wagon and mule that fall of 1861 to find another grist mill that would buy our crops. Every mill owner within ten miles or so of our farmstead turned us away because they heard that we stood foursquare for Lincoln. As we traveled from one village to another, Father didn't complain about our circumstances or my brothers' decision to join the Union army.

"I reckon they know what they're doin'," Father said.

It was toward the end of October when we came to the village of Kelley's Springs, some twenty miles or so from our farmstead. The village's grist mill owner told us that he would take our crops and he also told us that his village stood behind Lincoln. When Father and I came back home late the following day, we found Father's cousin, John Burden, at our farmstead. Everyone was happy to hear about our good fortune, and then cousin John told us that he was going to

Kentucky to join the Union army.

"I'd be a damn coward," Cousin John said, "if I didn't stand beside the Union flag and defend it."

"But Sarah and your boys need you," my mother said.

"Sarah knows why I'm wantin' to go."

"You can't expect Sarah to look after everythin'."

"Why not? She's looked after the farm whenever I've been away."

"That ain't the same as goin' off to war," my father said.

"I've set my mind to it, and that's it."

"Don't be muleheaded, John."

"I ain't muleheaded."

John said his goodbyes and left our farmstead. Some weeks later, Mother and I went to the Burden farmstead to deliver a couple of homespun shirts that she had made for Sarah Burden's two young sons.

"I'm plum scared out of my wits," Sarah said.

We told Sarah we would help her and her boys to look after the farm.

"It just weren't right he got up and left," she said.

Sarah told us the Vigilance Committee had come by the other day and told her the Burdens were on the blacklist because her husband had gone off to join the Union army.

"John was a fool for tellin' everybody what he was doin'," Sarah said.

"The war'll be over soon," Mother said, "and he'll come back."

"Why does he have to show off his courage just because there's a war?" Sarah asked. "Doesn't he know he's got enough courage just by lookin' after his family?"

Mother and I said our goodbyes to Sarah and her two sons and left the Burden farmstead. As we reached the end of the farm lane we looked back at the Burden farmhouse. Sarah was still standing on the front porch with her two young boys clinging tightly to her.

My brothers and I brought the last of our—and the Burdens'—crops to the grist mill in Kelley's Springs toward the end of November. After we came back, my brothers made themselves ready for the journey to Kentucky. The night before they were set to leave, Uncle George came to our farm. We thought he had come to ask us if we needed any dry goods, but instead, he told us with great anxiety that David and two other men had been caught by Confederate authorities while trying to burn down an old wooden bridge a day or so earlier some miles northeast of Hunleyville.

"They also killed a Confederate army soldier who was guardin' the bridge," he said, his voice shaking.

We could not believe it. All of us knew that David was high-spirited and rash, but surely he wasn't rash enough to burn a bridge or murder someone. *What in Heaven's name was David thinking?* I thought. My uncle told us that he knew nothing beforehand about his son's actions, but he knew that David wanted to fight the rebels any way he could. My uncle also told us that David and the two other men were in the courthouse jail waiting to appear before Judge Endicott for sentencing and that no one could see them. We tried our best to comfort my uncle, but he was overcome with worry and fear as he left our farmhouse.

Early the next morning, my cousin Henry came and told us that his brother and the two other men arrested with him would be sentenced at two o'clock that afternoon in the courthouse. We told Henry we would give the Paynters all the aid and comfort we could provide and that we would be at the courthouse to hear the sentencing.

My brothers stayed behind to look after our farm. We arrived in the village just before two o'clock and met my aunt, uncle, and cousin Henry in front of the courthouse. A large crowd had already gathered outside and many in the crowd gave us evil looks as we walked in. The small courtroom was filled with people, so we were forced to stand at the back. Many cruel-looking faces turned toward us, and we heard the words, "Traitor!" and "Yankee scum!" shouted in our direction. Two large wooden desks stood at the front of the courtroom. A young man whom I took to be the court scrivener sat behind one of the desks. He checked his pocket watch, looked at the wall clock, and then stood up.

"All rise! This court is now in session on this day, Friday, the twenty-ninth day of November 1861," he said. "The honorable Judge Samuel Benjamin Endicott presiding."

Judge Endicott, goateed and well-dressed, walked into the courtroom, sat down behind the other wooden desk, and struck his gavel. Everyone sat down. The courtroom fell silent.

"Our gallant Confederate Secretary of War, Mister Judah Benjamin," Judge Endicott said, "has issued instructions dated the twenty-fifth of this month to all courts in the Confederate state of Tennessee regarding the treatment of those caught in the recent bridge burnings in eastern Tennessee."

The judge cleared his throat and then continued speaking.

"These instructions apply to the three local men caught in the act of burning the Hunleyville bridge on the twenty-sixth of this month," the judge said, "and of murdering a brave Confederate soldier by the name of Ezekiel Thompson who stood watch on the bridge."

The young scrivener wrote with promptness.

"The secretary of war has instructed this court as follows," Judge Endicott said. "'All such as can be identified as having been engaged in bridge-burning are to be tried summarily by drumhead court-martial, and if found guilty, executed on the spot by hanging.'"

"Hurrah! We's goin' to have some hangings today!" somebody hollered.

Most of the folks in the courtroom cheered and applauded.

The courtroom guards brought in the first handcuffed and shackled prisoner. Goggle-eyed and sweating heavily, the man was jeered and laughed at by many in the courtroom. Judge Endicott read out loud the charges against the prisoner: destruction of Confederate property and the murder of a Confederate soldier.

"You have been found guilty of these charges," Judge Endicott said. "You will be hanged this afternoon at four o'clock, and your property will be seized and sold."

"But I've got a wife and children to look after!" the prisoner, wild-eyed, cried out.

"You should've thought of 'em before you did your burnin' and murderin,' you son of a b——h Yankee!" somebody yelled.

As the guards were taking him out of the courtroom, he again shouted, "I've got a wife and children to look after!"

Many people continued to laugh and jeer at him. The guards then brought in the second shackled and handcuffed prisoner. A mountain of a man. Many jeered him or called him all manner of vile names. The judge read out the same charges against him.

"You ain't nuthin' but a dirty coward!" the second prisoner shouted.

"I remind you, sir, that you are in a court of law," the judge said.

"I'll be damned if this is a court of law!" the second prisoner yelled. "You're the one who ought to get hanged, and I'll do the hangin' myself!"

"You have been found guilty of these charges," the judge said. "You will be hanged this afternoon at four o'clock, and your property will be seized and sold."

As the guards pulled him out of the courtroom, he shouted the foulest words imaginable at the judge.

Finally, the guards brought in my cousin, David, handcuffed and shackled. He shook like a leaf, and there were bruises on his face. Judge Endicott began to read out loud the charges against him.

"That boy ain't nuthin' but a dirty coward!" somebody cried out.

We shouted our support for David, but our voices were quickly drowned out by the hate-filled taunts from everybody else in the courtroom. My mother and Aunt Elizabeth clutched each other. I was terrified that the angry crowd in the courtroom would turn on us like a pack of wild dogs. Cheers broke out after Judge Endicott pronounced David's death sentence and the guards removed him from the courtroom.

"This court is now adjourned," Judge Endicott said and struck his gavel.

My aunt and my mother leaned on each other and cried as we walked back to my uncle's store. We suffered more snickers from passersby and some of them threw mud at us. We walked into the store, trudged upstairs to the family's quarters, and seated ourselves around the family table. No one said a word, and the only sound we heard was Aunt Elizabeth crying.

At the stroke of four o'clock that afternoon, Mother, Father, and

I stood with the Paynters a few steps away from the large crowd that had gathered by the gallows behind the courthouse. Three black coffins lay on the ground. The first prisoner who had appeared in front of Judge Endicott was brought out by the guards with his hands bound behind him. He was marched up the steps, a black hood was placed over his head, and a noose was put around his neck. Reverend Trumbull offered a short prayer, then the hooded hangman stepped forward and pulled the wooden lever. The prisoner fell through the trapdoor and struggled for a moment or two before his earthly life ended. The crowd cheered. His body hung for some minutes before the guards cut the rope, put his body into one of the coffins, loaded it onto a wagon, and drove it away.

The second prisoner who had stood in front of Judge Endicott was brought out, and his hands were also tied behind him. After he was marched up the steps, a black hood was placed over his head, and a noose was put around his neck and tightened. The reverend offered the same prayer and then the hooded hangman walked over to the wooden lever and pulled it. The second prisoner fell through the trapdoor and struggled for a moment or two before his life ended. The crowd cheered again. His body hung for some minutes before it was cut down and taken away.

David was the last one to be hanged. He was shaking like a leaf as he was brought out by the guards. With his hands bound behind him, he was marched up the steps. A black hood was put over his head and the noose was tightened around his neck. We prayed aloud as the reverend repeated his prayer. Then the hangman went up to the lever and pulled it. David fell through the trapdoor. The crowd cheered a third time as he struggled for a minute or so until two guards grabbed his legs, pulled him down, and ended his all-too-short life. My uncle and cousin Henry tried to comfort Aunt Elizabeth, but she was heartbroken. I felt deep sadness and heartfelt sorrow as the guards cut down David's body and took it away in a black coffin.

On the eighth of December 1861—my eighteenth birthday—my brothers left for Kentucky. My worries over what might happen to them in battle was mixed with bitterness over their forever denying me my long-held dream of working with horses. Father gave them our buckboard and one of our mares for the long journey. Mother gave them some food. John told us they would sell the horse and buckboard once they arrived in Kentucky and would send us the money by some means or other.

"It makes no matter," Father said.

Father and I shook hands with John and Charles and wished them Godspeed. Mother hugged each of my brothers and told them she would pray for them. John and Charles wished me a happy birthday before they climbed up onto the buckboard. John took hold of the reins and he and Charles looked at us for a moment before John snapped the reins. The voices of my father and mother and I shouting "God bless you!" followed them as they departed from our farmstead.

6

Barn Burners

On a cold and rain-swept day a week or so after my brothers left for Kentucky our neighbor Samuel Tyrrell's two younger sons, Otis and Emmett, rode up to our farm on a pair of mud-splattered horses. While Mother stayed inside, Father and I stepped out onto the front porch as they got off their mounts. They wore dirty slouch hats, and their pants, boots, and the bottom edges of their tattered black coats were sprayed with mud. Emmett unbuttoned his coat to reveal a leather holster on his right hip that held a long-barreled Colt Army pistol.

"We've come to tell you we ran the Paynters off last night," Emmett said.

"And they ain't comin' back," Otis said.

A smile spread across Otis's flat, ugly, scraggly-bearded face, revealing broken, tobacco-stained teeth.

"Why'd you run 'em off?" Father asked.

"They were causin' us nuthin' but trouble," Emmett said.

"Where'd they get run off to?" I asked.

"Georgia," Otis said.

Father and I glanced at each other.

"Judge Endicott's wantin' you Meechams to take the oath,"

Emmett said, "so he can strike your names off the blacklist."

"Sounds like a fair trade," Otis said. "What d'you say, Meecham?"

"Who else has taken the oath?" I asked.

"Most everybody who's on the list has taken it," Emmett said.

"And they ain't on the list no more," Otis said.

"What've they said 'bout takin' the oath?" Father asked.

"They ain't said a damn word," Emmett said. "They just got over to the courthouse, swore out the oath, and got back to where they come from."

"We ain't takin' any rebel oath," Father said.

Emmett sighed, took off his hat, ran one of his dirty hands through his long, greasy hair, put his hat back on his head, and rested his right hand on the butt of his Colt pistol. Otis's reptile-like black eyes darted back and forth between Father and me.

"The judge ain't goin' to like it," Emmett said.

"That's for sure," Otis said. "He ain't goin' to like it one damn bit," and he shook his head.

The Tyrrell brothers got up on their mounts and rode away. Father and I went into our farmhouse and told Mother what had happened to the Paynters.

"Poor Elizabeth, and George, and poor Henry!" Mother said. "Haven't they suffered enough?"

It was a couple of days or so after the Tyrrell brothers' visit that the barn burnings began. Father and I were walking to our barn early one morning to feed the livestock when we saw a mile or so away a tall, dark plume of smoke rising into the sky.

"There's somethin' goin' on at Silas Ewell's farm," I said.

The Ewells—Silas, his wife, Martha, and their children—were decent, honest, and law-abiding people, and our dearest friends and neighbors. I bridled two of our horses and hitched them to our wagon while Father ran back to the farmhouse. He soon returned with his Springfield musket and climbed up into the wagon seat beside me.

"We might be needin' it," Father said. "I told your mother what's happened. She's afraid, but I told her not to worry."

We drove as fast as we could to the Ewell farmstead. By the time we arrived, Silas's barn had burned to the ground and the smell of burning animal flesh hung heavy in the air.

"It was the screamin' that woke us," Silas said. "I got up and saw the barn on fire. Martha and the girls were scared somethin' awful. I told them to stay inside. I ran outside, but I couldn't do anythin'. It was too late."

"Did you see anyone 'round the barn?" I asked.

Silas, his face creased and thickly bearded, shook his head.

"Mighty sorry 'bout your barn, Silas," Father said, "and a real shame 'bout your livestock."

"I figure I'll just start over again," Silas said.

Father told Silas that we would help him build a new barn and give him some of our livestock to help him with his farming. Silas was much relieved and thanked us for our help.

"This is a warnin' for us Lincoln men," Father said. "Next time, they'll be comin' to kill us."

On the afternoon of Christmas Eve, we saw another plume of dark smoke rising over another farm a half-mile or so away, and we knew it was the homestead of Father's cousin, John Burden, and his family.

"William, can't we leave?" Mother asked. "It's too dangerous for us here! Please, William, we've got to leave!"

Father told her to pray until he and I came back from the Burdens. Father took his rifle and we drove our wagon and horses as fast as we could to the Burden farmstead. We arrived to see the barn completely on fire. A pair of horses had escaped from the burning barn and they were on fire as they dashed about on the muddy farm fields. Sarah and her young sons, Billy and Franklin, stood on the front porch of their farmhouse. Sarah was weeping. As soon as we jumped off our wagon, Father ran over to the porch to comfort Sarah and her boys, while I took Father's rifle and ran into the farm fields to put the poor horses out of their misery. I finished my sad work and ran back to the Burden farmhouse.

"I told him they'd be comin' after us!" Sarah wailed. "I told him he ought to have stayed here!"

"John did what he knew was right," Father said.

"It wasn't right!" Sarah cried. "I told him he shouldn't go! We've lost everythin'!"

Father told me we had to take Sarah and her boys to another farmstead for their protection.

"We'll take them over to the Mooney farm," Father said. "That's the safest place for 'em."

Father and I helped Sarah and her sons gather up some of their belongings and headed for the Mooney farm some five miles or so away. We soon arrived at the Mooneys' farmstead and told Augustus Mooney, his rosy-cheeked wife, Mary, and their three tall sons what had happened at the Burden farm. Augustus, tall and muscular, told us they had seen the black smoke. Father told me to help the Burdens get settled and then get myself home as quickly as I could, while he went back to our farmstead because he did not want to leave Mother alone. I watched Father leave and then I helped the Burdens unpack their belongings. As dusk was falling, Augustus brought out a bridled and saddled young chestnut mare from his barn.

"Her name's Sugar 'cause she's got a sweet temper," Augustus said, handing me the reins. "She's well watered, rested, and fed. Just give her the reins."

I said goodbye to everyone and spurred Sugar back to our farmstead. I galloped back along the same country roads that Father and I and the Burdens had traveled along earlier that day. I pulled up on Sugar's reins when I reached the top of a rise in the rough road and saw in the near distance three horsemen—Hiram Boldt and the two younger Tyrrell brothers—astride the road. I turned Sugar into the surrounding woods, pulled up on the reins, and dismounted. I stroked her neck, hoping—and praying—that she would not make a sound.

I watched through the leafless trees as Hiram Boldt and the Tyrrell brothers trotted up the dirt road and halted their horses not ten yards from where I had entered the woods. One of their horses snorted and one of the horsemen coughed loudly before they turned their mounts around and trotted back down the road in the gathering gloom. I waited for a while before I led Sugar out of the woods and onto the dirt road. I got up onto the saddle and rode slowly because I was afraid those three horsemen were lying in wait for me somewhere up ahead.

I soon reached the top of another rise in the road. A half-mile or so ahead a farm was burning brightly. Thick black smoke and glowing orange-and-yellow flames were rising into the sky.

"Oh God, no!" I cried out.

I whipped Sugar with the reins and kept whipping her as I rode past Stoneman's Wood toward the burning farmstead. I jumped off

Sugar as soon as we turned into the farm lane. Terrified, I hobbled up the farm lane to my family's farmhouse. Everything was in flames. One of our plowing mules and a milking cow were on fire, and both of them were screaming and running wildly around the farm fields. In front of our burning farmhouse, my father lay on the ground by our wagon, his body filled with fearsome bullet holes. The wagon's pair of horses had been shot dead, and they lay on the ground tangled up in their bridles and reins. I looked over at our burning farmhouse and saw my mother lying on the front porch. I ran over to her. Her face was badly bruised and bloody, and she had been shot many times.

Surrounded by death, fire, and clouds of smoke, I was overcome with shock and fright. I stumbled off the farmhouse steps and saw two dark figures sitting astride a pair of horses in the farm field that lay directly behind our farmhouse. Still filled with fear and in shock, I somehow collected myself and hobbled back down the farm lane to Sugar. She stood where I had left her. I climbed up into the saddle, whipped her sides with the reins, and galloped off.

I rode along the country road for a distance before I reined Sugar into Stoneman's Wood. Crashing through the undergrowth and snapping off small tree branches in the thick, darkening woods, I dared not look back until we safely reached a deep and muddy ravine on the far side of the forest. I pulled up on Sugar's reins and looked back over my shoulder. Not a soul was seen. Not a sound was heard. I got out of the saddle, tied Sugar's reins to a nearby tree branch, laid myself down on the cold, hard ground, and covered myself with old leaves and small branches. No sooner had I done so than my shock and fear gave way to an immense grief. I wept until I fell into a fitful sleep.

I awoke on Christmas Day. Darkness was beating a slow retreat as a pale morning light was beginning to spread across the sky from the east. I glanced at Sugar. She was eating hickory nuts that lay on the ground near a large hickory tree. As I lay shivering, sore, hungry, and alone, I swore a blood vengeance against Hiram Boldt.

7

SANCTUARY

My Christmas Day meal was a handful of hickory nuts, and I quenched my thirst with a handful of snow. By late afternoon I was determined to find food and water. I untied Sugar's reins from the tree branch and we tramped along a rough trail to the southernmost edge of Stoneman's Wood where Obadiah Adkins's farm stood. I knew that Obadiah was a Confederate, but I hoped that he still had a measure of regard for me that would move him to give me a few provisions.

My hopes were dashed, however, when I saw mounted riders, among them Hiram Boldt and the two younger Tyrrell brothers, in front of Obadiah's farmhouse. Obadiah was standing on the front porch and was pointing toward Stoneman's Wood. I knew at that moment that I had to flee. My only hope of sanctuary now was Augustus Mooney's farmhouse. I tramped back with Sugar to last night's resting spot and then led her along another rough trail that led to the northeastern most edge of Stoneman's Wood and the country road that led to the Mooney farm five miles or so away.

Twilight was falling as I got up into the saddle and spurred Sugar. She galloped for three miles or so before she began to slow down. I got down and led her by the reins. No sooner had I done so than

I heard the sound of horse hoofs some distance behind me, and I cursed my luck. I got back up onto Sugar and spurred her again. The thought crossed my mind of turning off into the woods and hiding there until the danger passed, but I felt that my luck would not hold this time. After cantering for two miles or so, Sugar brought me to a crossroads. I knew I was close to Augustus Mooney's farmstead. As I reined her eastward along the country road that led toward the Mooney homestead, I saw not twenty yards ahead two Confederate bushwhackers sitting on their horses, with long-barreled rifles slung across their backs, and holstered revolvers on their hips.

"Who the hell are you?" one of them shouted.

I spurred Sugar into the woods and heard the *crack!* of a revolver firing. A bullet hummed past my head like a hornet and slammed into a tree. *Crack!* Another bullet flew past my left arm and clipped a tree branch as I rode past it. I spurred Sugar deeper into the woods until darkness fell. I pulled up on the reins, got off Sugar, and spent a sleepless night in the woods.

At first light, I arose exhausted and weak but determined to make my way to the Mooney farm. I led Sugar through the woods to the dirt road where I had encountered the two Confederate partisans, and we plodded along the road for a time until we reached the Mooney homestead. I was overcome with relief as we tramped up the farm lane, and I was elated to see Augustus Mooney standing on the front porch of his farmhouse. When he caught sight of me, he ran over to me, and we embraced.

"James, everybody thought you were dead!" he said.

We took Sugar to the barn and then went into the farmhouse. Augustus's wife, Mary, hugged me and their sons shook my hand. Mary brought me some food and water, and I ate and drank my fill.

Augustus told me that Silas Ewell had come by late on Christmas Day and told them that he heard that Confederate partisans had laid waste to the Meecham farmstead after murdering my father, my mother, and me. I told them everything that happened after I left their farm on Christmas Eve.

"God bless your father and mother, James," Mary said, tears welling up in her eyes. "They were good people."

I told them how I had made my way back to their farmstead and my encounter with a pair of Confederate bushwhackers.

"They came by last night," Augustus said. "We shot at 'em and scared 'em away, but they'll be back. And they'll bring others with 'em. They're murderin' anyone who's for Lincoln."

He told me that he was taking his family to a man he knew well and trusted, a farmer by the name of Virgil Huff, who lived near the village of Kelley's Springs.

"We've got to leave," Augustus said, "We ain't got no choice."

He told me that Sarah Burden and her two sons had left for Kelley's Springs on Christmas Day.

"We're leavin' at first light," Augustus said, "and you're comin' with us."

Augustus and his family were set on getting themselves to Kelley's Springs, but I wasn't. I was grateful to the Mooney family for giving me a safe harbor in which to shelter, but it pained me deeply to leave behind my family's homestead for an unknown future. I told Augustus how I felt.

"I've got to get back to my family's farm."

"You can't go back."

"Why can't I?"

"Rebels will kill you quick as they lay eyes on you."

"But I've got to bury my father and mother."

"The Good Lord's lookin' after 'em now."

I started to protest, but Augustus raised his hand.

"Best you get some sleep," he said. "We're leavin' at first light."

Augustus told his sons to get some hay from the barn. After I finished eating my victuals, Augustus took me to the root cellar underneath their farmhouse. The smell of vegetables hung thick in the cold damp air. Mary followed us with a pile of blankets. Augustus's sons returned with bundles of hay. They spread the hay on the rough dirt floor and Mary laid the blankets on top. I lay down on the roughly made bed and, in the next moment, I fell asleep.

I had a fitful sleep. I dreamt of Mother standing on the front porch of our burning farmhouse with a look of what I took to be terror on her face, calling out my father's name. I woke up in a cold sweat. I tossed and turned for a time before I fell asleep again. I dreamt of Father and I hunting in Stoneman's Wood. We came to a worm fence and Father climbed over it, but I couldn't because of my somewhat shorter left leg. I called out to him for help, but he disappeared into the woods. Just before I woke up, Charlotte appeared to me in my final dream.

"Where is he?" she kept saying.

I shook myself awake. Augustus was standing over me and was holding a lit lantern in his hand.

"Best you get up now, James," he said. "My boys have taken our livestock to Kelley's Springs, and we'll be leavin' soon. Looks like we're in for a spell of rain."

I got up and followed him upstairs. Mary gave me hot biscuits and warm coffee. After I ate and drank my fill, I told Augustus that I needed to write to my brothers in Kentucky and tell them what had happened at our family's farmstead. He gave me some paper, a plain envelope, and the stub of a pencil, and I sat down at their rough-hewn table.

> Near Kelley's Springs, Tennessee
> December 27, 1861
>
> Dearest John and Charles,
> A terrible thing happened Christmas Eve. Our farm
> was burned down and our livestock was all killed by
> Hiram Boldt and his bunch of rebel bushwhackers.
> Father and mother are dead. It was also Hiram Boldt
> and his bunch that did this terrible thing. They near
> killed me. They is burning everything and killing any-
> one who is for Lincoln. I got myself to the Mooney
> farm. All of us is going to a farmer by the name of
> Virgil Huff out by Kelley's Springs.
>
> James

I put the letter inside the envelope and sealed it, wrote my brothers' names on it, and gave the envelope to Augustus. I needed to get some fresh air, so I limped out onto the front porch of the farmhouse and was overjoyed to see my cousin, Henry, and Silas Ewell, his wife, Martha, and their two daughters.

"Augustus came by our place last night," Silas said, "and told us you were alive, and we gave thanks to the Almighty!"

"We're all broken-hearted 'bout your father and mother," Martha said.

I shook Silas's hand and hugged Martha and their daughters, and then I looked at Henry.

"Thank God you're still alive!" I cried out as I hugged him.

I was shocked by Henry's appearance—his face pale and thin, and his clothes filthy and tattered. He told us that Hiram Boldt and the Tyrrell brothers—Emmett and Otis—had dragged him and his father and mother out of their store one night at gunpoint and handed them over to two armed Confederate army soldiers. The soldiers forced them into a wagon, Henry told us.

"When I asked 'em where they were takin' us," Henry said, "they said we were goin' to a Confederate prison in Georgia 'cause we were Southern traitors who stood for that Black Republican Lincoln."

From time to time the two rebel soldiers would halt the wagon to eat or drink and look after the two mules that were pulling the wagon, Henry told us, but he and his father and mother were given nothing to drink or eat. It was near the Georgia state line, Henry told us, that the Confederate soldiers stopped the wagon again, and in that moment his mother and father told him to save himself.

"I jumped out of the wagon," Henry said, "and I ran off into the nearby woods."

One of the Confederate soldiers ran after him, Henry told us, but he was too slow and gave up the chase after some time.

"I walked for days through the woods," Henry said, "before I finally got myself to Mister Ewell's place early this morning."

He trembled for a moment and looked away. "I shouldn't have left 'em behind," he said and shook his head.

I told him his mother and father had saved him from dying in some godforsaken rebel prison in Georgia.

"I should've stayed with 'em," he said.

Tears began to run down his dirty, unshaven cheeks. He stepped off the porch and stumbled toward the barn. I started to follow him, but Silas called out to me.

"Let 'im be, James," he said. "The Good Lord's testin' his faith."

I knew God was also testing my faith.

Our small train of two wagons left for Kelley's Springs on the twenty-seventh day of December 1861. A cold rain mixed with sleet fell straight and hard. Filled with a burdensome depression of spirits, I sat beside Augustus in his wagon seat and held onto his ancient musket. Augustus's wife, Mary, sat wrapped in blankets in the wagon box. Canvas sheets covered their simple belongings. My horse Sugar was tied by her reins to the wagon and was pulled along at a trot. The Ewells and my cousin, Henry, followed us in their wagon. We journeyed along country roads that led through wet and leafless woods, past barren farm fields, and the scattered remains of scorched farmhouses and barns. The weathered wagon's ungreased wood and metal sharply creaked and clattered, and the mules' harnesses jingled.

"We've got to trust in the Almighty, James," Augustus said.

His voice, it seemed to me, was miles away.

8

WAR DRUMS

The rain and sleet ended by the time we reached Kelley's Springs late that afternoon. We halted in front of the village's two-story, wooden-clapboard general store. A sign over its front doors read, "Zachariah Foley, Proprietor." As Henry and I were tying up the mules to a couple of hitching posts, we heard shouts.

"James! Henry!"

We saw Jedediah Woodson, Absalom Johnson, and Father's cousin-in-law, Sarah Burden, hurrying along the wooden-planked sidewalk toward us. They were overjoyed to see us and we all embraced.

"Thanks be to God that you're alive!" Absalom cried out.

After they said their helloes to our travel companions—the Ewell and Mooney families—Henry and I told them about our harrowing experiences. Jedediah and Absalom shook their heads and had sorrowful looks on their faces, and Sarah shed more than a few tears.

"Lean on the Almighty," Jedediah said, his voice shaking. "He is your rock."

Absalom and Sarah nodded. Absalom told us that he was working at the village livery stable. Jedediah said that he was employed at the village barrel maker's shop. Sarah told us that she was helping the village dressmaker and was living with her two sons in a small room above the shop. Absalom asked Henry and me if we had a place to stay, and we told him we were following the Ewells and the Mooneys to some local farmers' homesteads.

"You'll stay with me," Absalom said. "There's a couple of rope beds and a spare room where I'm staying at the livery stable."

We told the Mooneys and the Ewells about our new living quarters, and Silas Ewell said that he would pay us a visit in the morning. Jedediah promised us breakfast. We said our goodbyes to everyone and followed Absalom to the livery stable.

As he had promised, Jedediah brought us breakfast the next morning and we ate and drank our fill. It was near ten o'clock when Silas came with a shabbily dressed farmer. Silas introduced Samuel Clay to us, and then Silas asked Henry and me how we were faring. We told him we were faring as best we could.

"There's a meetin' tonight at Foley's store," Samuel said, "for folks who're wantin' to fight rebels. The Union army sure ain't doin' no fightin' 'round these parts."

"We ain't got no choice," Silas said. "We've got to fight 'em."

Silas invited Jedediah, Henry, and me to the meeting.

"The n——r ain't welcome," Samuel said. He pointed his forefinger at Jedediah and shook his head.

"Why not?" Silas asked.

"A n——r ain't worth a damn when it comes to fightin'," Samuel said.

I asked Samuel how he had come to know this, and he told me it was taken as gospel by many people around this part of the county.

"I ain't ever run away from a fight," Jedediah said.

"His kind's always skedaddlin' when there's fightin' that needs doin'," Samuel said.

Jedediah took a step toward Samuel.

"I'll show you who skedaddles when there's fightin' to be done," Jedediah muttered.

He leaned in close to Samuel's face and gave him a cold, hard look. Samuel stood stock-still for a moment, and then he turned and walked over to the other side of the room. I had no doubt that Jedediah would have given him a mighty good licking if Samuel had given him half a chance.

After some time passed, the atmosphere had eased enough for me to tell Silas that I wanted to settle accounts with every Confederate. Henry told us that he felt the same way.

"I want to send 'em to hell!" Henry shouted.

We met many local farmers and villagers at the meeting that night in Foley's store. Abraham Mooney introduced us to a bearded, scruffy-looking Virgil Huff and his gangly son, Robert. Virgil told me that he would take my letter—along with a bunch of letters from other farmers and villagers—the next morning to a Union army camp in Kentucky. I wished him a hearty Godspeed. During the meeting, farmers and villagers spoke out against the rebel partisans who had been raiding farms around Kelley's Springs.

"A couple of 'em rode up to my place a day or so ago," one farmer said, "and tried to burn down my farmhouse. I shot at 'em and scared 'em off, but I can't fight off all of 'em by myself."

"I ain't slept since I got told by 'em that they was wantin' to get me and my family off our land," another farmer said.

Silas Ewell proposed that a Union-mounted outfit be set up to defend the village of Kelley's Springs and every local farmer who supported President Lincoln. A vote was called, and all of us voted in favor. Some twenty-five farmers and villagers—including Jedediah, my cousin Henry, Robert Huff, Samuel Clay, Silas Ewell, and I—signed our names or made our marks on the new outfit's muster roll. Silas was democratically elected as our leader. Samuel Clay proposed that the outfit be called "Ewell's Rangers," and all of us voted in favor.

Jedediah, Henry, and I thanked those local farmers and villagers who had given us some of their firearms because we had none of our own. Those who chose not to join up—they had young families or they felt they were too old to fight—told us they would give us provisions and safe shelter and inform us about any movements of local Confederate army units or rebel partisan outfits.

I filled the few remaining days in December with daily work at the village livery stable, but my nights were filled with loneliness, heartache, anger, and bitterness. Sleep was fitful as I spent my nights brooding over my fate, and I felt that God had simply abandoned me. I received no letters from my brothers and wondered endlessly what had become of them. Henry, lost in his own thoughts, was sullen the entire time. He shared no thoughts and few words with me, and I, in turn, shared nothing of my inner demons with him. Jedidiah, Absalom, and Sarah Burden tried to raise our spirits as New Year's Eve came and went, but Henry and I had no reason to celebrate. New Year's Day shone clear and bright and held out the hope that better days might yet come.

Ewell's Rangers rode into rebel territory for the first time on a cold and snowy January morning in early 1862. We gathered with our mounts, our firearms, and our provisions at the village's livery stable. Local farmers had told us that the Confederate army had built two stout log cabin outposts a half-mile apart on the banks of two large creeks—Black Locust Creek and Anvil Creek—some three miles or so north of Kelley's Springs. Confederate cavalrymen from those two outposts had been seen riding with a small band of Confederate guerrillas on their frequent raids around Crawford's Mill, a hamlet five miles or so north of Kelley's Springs.

"I can't wait to give 'em a damn good lickin'," Robert Huff said.

Silas Ewell chose a dozen of us—including Jedediah, Robert Huff, and me—and told us that we would attack the first outpost that stood on the south bank of Black Locust Creek. Samuel Clay would lead the remainder of Ewell's Rangers—including my cousin Henry—and attack the other outpost further north near Anvil Creek. Silas then told us that our two groups would join up at Crawford's Mill after attacking the two outposts.

"We'll give 'em a chance to surrender," Silas said. "But if they want to fight, we'll send 'em to hell!"

Silas and the other rangers whooped and hollered, but I didn't join in. While I was still filled with a burning hatred for Hiram Boldt and his fellow rebel partisans, I was also troubled by the feeling that I might turn tail and run away from a fight. I condemned myself for lacking courage, but the feeling of cowardice became even more firmly rooted in my mind. The cheering died down and we made ready to ride out of the village.

We followed snowy forest trails and crossed several wooded hollers before we came to Black Locust Creek. We got off our horses and crept through the thick leafless woods. Small tree branches snapped and cracked as we tramped through the forest. We halted inside the woods several yards away from the edge of a man-made clearing. Some forty yards away stood a flat-roofed, windowless, thick-logged cabin surrounded by scattered tree stumps. Smoke curled upward from its chimney. Ten horses stood tethered to a picket line near the cabin. No Confederates stood guard. As I stared at the log cabin and the chimney smoke, a sudden spasm of courage overcame my cowardly feelings. I trudged over to Silas.

"I'll smoke 'em out," I whispered.

Silas looked at me for a moment and nodded.

"All right," he whispered. "But be mighty careful."

I tramped back to Sugar and swung up into the saddle. I guided her through the woods and across the clearing, and all the while my heart was beating furiously. I pulled up on the reins as soon as we came up to the side of the cabin where the chimney poked out of the flat roof. I pulled out a rolled-up sheet of canvas from my saddlebag, stood up on the saddle, and climbed up onto the roof. After I unrolled the sheet, I draped it over the chimney and jumped off the roof. I walked around to the front of the cabin, unholstered my pistol, and cocked the hammer. My mouth was as dry as a bone and my pistol hand shook as I pointed my Colt at the front door. Smoke began to seep through the cracks in the door and it swung open. A bearded, rough-looking Confederate soldier stood in the doorway coughing and holding a revolver. And then he saw me.

"What the hell d'you think you're doin'?" he shouted.

I pulled the trigger and my revolver erupted. The Confederate soldier fell backward into the cabin. My revolver hand shook terribly as I got myself over to Sugar, grabbed her reins, and limped back into the forest with her in tow.

Inside those same woods, the rest of Silas Ewell's men were kneeling behind tree trunks and leafless bushes pointing their firearms at the cabin. A small group of Confederate army soldiers—coughing loudly and armed with muskets and revolvers—stumbled out of the smoke-filled cabin and formed a rough half-circle in front of it. Silas called out to them to surrender their arms and their persons.

"We ain't surrenderin' to no damn Yankees!" a Confederate soldier yelled back, and they fired off a ragged volley at us.

A couple of bullets clipped tree branches, some slammed into trees, but others hit their marks. A ranger who was kneeling beside me was shot in the head and fell. Another ranger dropped his musket after he was shot in the throat. He stood up clutching his throat and staggered backward into the woods until he fell over a large fallen tree branch.

"Be strong in the Lord," Silas cried out to us, "and in the power of His might!"

Silas, a righteous and God-fearing man, carried a small Bible with him wherever he went. He read it devoutly every day, but he also had the irritating habit of shouting out biblical sayings to anyone who came within earshot, regardless of whether or not they were filled with the Holy Spirit.

The Confederates fired off another ragged volley at us and another ranger fell.

"Give 'em hell, boys!" Silas shouted at us.

We fired our muskets once, reloaded, and fired again. I trembled as I fired my musket and my revolver. Confederate soldiers fell in bunches as our bullets struck them. They fired off another scattered volley at us while we reloaded, but none of us were hit. We fired off our muskets again, and at that instant, I beheld through the hazy gun smoke a truly horrible sight. A young Confederate soldier, a gaping red hole with bits of bone and shreds of blackened flesh where his mouth and jaw had once been, stumbled toward me. I watched, transfixed and horrified, as the poor soul fell upon his hands and knees and crawled away toward the far side of the clearing.

Silas kept shouting, "Give 'em hell, boys!" as we fired volley after volley at the Confederates.

The rebels soon stopped shooting at us. Silas shouted for us to stop firing and we knew the battle was over. Those of us who had survived this fight stood up and walked through the gun smoke toward the cabin. I was still shaking and dared not look at any of the dead and mortally wounded Confederate soldiers who lay on the bloody, snow-covered ground. Several rangers whooped as they gathered up Confederate pistols, muskets, and cartridge boxes. Other rangers ran into the cabin and plundered it.

Jedediah shot two Confederate horses that had been badly wounded by our firings, and he untied the remaining horses from the picket line and herded them away from the cabin. I turned my back to the field of battle and hobbled into the woods for a short distance before I stopped, leaned over, and retched. I was still emptying my stomach when Silas found me.

"You showed real grit, James," Silas said.

"But I killed a man!"

"Ain't no shame in killin' a rebel."

"There's plenty of shame for me."

I retched again and wiped my mouth. My stomach ached, my legs felt wobbly, and I was shaking.

"We're fightin' for the Union, James."

"I ain't fightin' no more for the Union."

"Hell and damnation! Have you forgotten what those rebels did to your folks?"

"I ain't forgotten."

"They're burnin' farms and murderin' anyone who's against

'em."

My head was pounding like a war drum.

"We're God's avenging sword!" Silas shouted. "Thus saith the Prophet Ezekiel, 'Ye have feared the sword; and I will bring a sword upon you, saith the Lord God.'"

I retched again.

"We'd better get back to the others, James," Silas said.

I groaned, wiped my mouth, and straightened up. Silas held me by the arm as we trudged back to the clearing.

We buried the dead on both sides, set fire to the log cabin, mounted our horses, and plodded through the snow-filled woods until we reached the muddy road that ran between Kelley's Springs and Crawford's Mill. We rode north until we reached Crawford's Mill and met up with Samuel Clay, Henry, and the rest of Ewell's Rangers.

While we rested on our mounts and ate our simple provisions, Jedediah and I told my cousin Henry about our tussle. Henry told us that he and the others had not met any Confederate soldiers at the Anvil Creek outpost, but they had tussled with a handful of Confederate bushwhackers just south of Crawford's Mill. He pointed to a thin, scruffy, and homely-looking young rebel who was sitting on a horse nearby with his hands tied behind him. A ranger, sitting astride his horse, was pointing his pistol at the Confederate.

"We caught this rebel bushwhacker hidin' behind a tree," Henry said and laughed.

Silas reined his horse up to the young Confederate prisoner.

"Seems like I ought to know you," Silas said.

A smirk spread across the rebel's ugly face.

"You're Walter Tidewell, ain't you?" Silas asked.

"So what if I is?" the Confederate said.

"You're him, all right," Silas said. "I'd know that ugly face anywheres. You worked for Josiah McHenry at his grist mill over in Hunleyville, didn't you?"

"So what if I did?" Walter said.

"What're you doin' in these parts?" Silas asked.

Walter shrugged.

"Been doin' plenty of burnin' and killin', haven't you?" Silas asked.

Walter's smirk disappeared and his eyes widened.

"I ain't done nuthin' like that," Walter spluttered.

"Ain't you been ridin' with those rebel raiders?" Samuel asked.

"I done rode with 'em," Walter said, "but that don't mean I done any burnin' or killin' like you said I done."

Silas leaned in close to Walter's face.

"You're sellin' us nuthin' but a bill of goods," Silas said.

"No, sir, I ain't sellin' you a bill of goods," Walter said, his voice trembling. "It's me that got sold a bill of goods!"

"How'd that happen?" I asked.

"My pa told me I had to join them bushwhackers 'cause they was defendin' our land," Walter said, his voice still trembling. "Otherwise he'd beat me somethin' awful like he done sometimes. So, I done what he told me, and everythin' was fine 'til all the shootin' started. Then I got plenty scared!"

"Well, what d'you know," Jedediah said. "A yellow rebel." He laughed.

"That's right," Walter said. "I ain't nuthin' but a plain, simple coward 'cause I'm just plain scared of fightin' anybody."

"If you's a coward," Samuel said, "why'd they let you ride with 'em?"

"I told 'em I was mighty good at lookin' after horses and cattle," Walter said. "So, they got me roundin' up all the horses and cattle we could find, and I'd sell 'em to the Confederate army."

"Sounds like a nice profitable business," Henry said. "How d'you get your hands on these cattle and horses?"

"We helped ourselves to 'em every time we paid a visit to a Yankee farmer," Walter said, and a smirk spread again across his ugly face.

"Hell and damnation!" Silas cried out. "You ain't no better than the rest of 'em! I oughta just hang you!"

Walter's face turned pale, and he began to shake terribly.

"No, please, sir, please don't hang me!" Walter cried out. "I ain't done no burnin' or killin'!"

"Somebody get me a rope!" Samuel hollered.

A ranger pulled out a coil of rope from his saddlebag and tossed it to Samuel. Walter struggled to free his hands.

"I'm mighty good at takin' care of horses!" Walter cried out. "I swear that's all I've ever done!"

"Let's hang 'im so every rebel will know what's waitin' for 'im!" Robert Huff hollered.

"I ain't got nuthin' against Yankees! I swear I don't! Mister Ewell, sir, please, sir, I can help you, sir. I swear I can!"

"Give me that rope!" Robert yelled. "I'll hang 'im myself!"

Samuel tossed the coiled rope to Robert and he began to tie a noose.

"Please, sir, I'll tell you who's been leadin' them bushwhackers! I'll take you to 'em! Just please don't hang me, sir!"

Robert reined his horse up to Walter and yanked him off his horse. He threw the noose around Walter's scrawny neck as he lay on the ground and pulled it snug. As Walter struggled to get up, he soiled himself.

"Well, look at what we've got here," Henry said. "A dirty yellow rebel." He laughed.

Samuel, Robert, Jedediah, and the other rangers joined Henry in laughing at Walter, and they jeered him, but I felt only pity for the wretched and shabbily dressed creature kneeling in the mud and snow. He sobbed for a while, and then he told us that a farmer by the name of Isham Hagerman was the local rebel leader and that it was Isham Hagerman and the other Confederate partisans who had cruelly left him behind after tussling with us just outside of Crawford's Mill.

"Where'd Hagerman and the others ride off to?" I asked.

"We've got... I mean... They've got a hideaway," Walter muttered.

"Where is it?" I asked.

Walter shook his head. "I can't tell you," he said. "I just can't tell you." He shook his head again.

"You just told us you'd take us to 'em," Henry said.

"I... I can't tell you," he said.

"I swear we'll hang you right here and now, Walter, if you don't tell us!" Silas shouted.

Walter glanced at Silas, lowered his head, and began to weep.

Late that afternoon, Samuel Clay and a half-dozen rangers—including Jedediah, Henry, Robert Huff, and I—rode along snowy dirt roads with a soiled Walter in tow to the Hagerman hideout that Walter had told us was some five miles northeast of Crawford's Mill. Silas and the other rangers stayed behind in case any Confederate partisans or Confederate army soldiers came back to the hamlet. As we rode toward Hagerman's lair, I was sweating heavily and my heart beat kept rising higher and higher until I thought it was in my throat.

We soon reached the farmstead, got down off our horses, and pulled out our pistols and rifles. Two rangers stayed behind to watch the horses and guard Walter. The rest of us climbed over a worm fence. We crossed a snow-covered farm field toward a broken-down farmhouse. As we approached it, Jedediah and Robert broke off from our group. Jedediah walked up to one corner of the homestead and Robert walked up to the other corner, and they both stood watch. As Samuel, Henry, and I came up to the broken porch steps, the front door opened a crack.

"What the hell d'you want?" someone shouted from inside the farmhouse.

"We're lookin' for Isham Hagerman!" Samuel yelled.

The door opened wide. A young farm boy stepped out onto the porch pointing a long-barreled mountain rifle at us. He slowly walked across the porch to the top of the porch steps and stopped. A tall, grizzled man followed close behind him, also carrying a long-barreled mountain rifle.

"I reckon you'd be the feller we're lookin' for," Samuel said.

"What the hell d'you mean trespassin' on my land!" Isham Hagerman growled.

He lifted his rifle, cocked the hammer, and aimed it at Samuel.

"You've been burnin' Union farms," I said. My heart was still in my throat.

"And killin' Union farmers," Henry said.

"That ain't nuthin' but a bunch of goddamn lies," Isham muttered. "I ain't burned nuthin', and I sure as hell ain't killed nobody."

"You're a liar, Hagerman," Samuel said.

Jedediah and Robert stepped backward as a pair of rough-looking Confederates appeared from behind the farmhouse pointing their revolvers at them.

"We're here to settle accounts with you," Samuel said.

"We'll settle 'em all right!" Isham hollered.

His mountain rifle erupted. The shot hit Samuel square in the face and knocked him backward onto the ground. Henry fired off his pistol at Isham, and Isham collapsed. The farm boy on the porch fired off his mountain rifle at me but missed, and I fired off my Colt pistol at him and he fell down the porch steps. I heard shots and looked over at Jedediah. He had shot dead the rebel partisan who had been facing him. I looked over at Robert. He was staggering back toward Henry and me, and his right arm was bleeding. Robert had shot the bushwhacker who had been confronting him, and that rebel now lay dead face down in the mud and snow. The shoot-out was over.

My heart was still in my throat and my shirt was soaked in sweat as Henry and I walked over to Samuel's body. He had no face. I stripped off the jacket from the dead rebel who lay on the ground in front of Jedediah and wrapped it around Samuel's head, and Jedediah and Henry carried him back to our horses. I held Robert by his good arm and we followed them. After we laid Samuel's body over his horse's saddle and got Robert up onto his horse, Jedediah and I went back to the farmhouse and plundered it of all the firearms we could find. We returned to our mounts and made our way back to Crawford's Mill.

Ewell's Rangers rode back to Kelley's Springs late that evening. The next day we helped Samuel Clay's family bury him in the village's small cemetery and comforted them and the other families who had lost loved ones during the fight at the Black Locust Creek clearing. We recruited a couple of new rangers and Walter Tidewell was put to work in the village livery stable under the watchful eye of Absalom Johnson.

Sometime after Robert Huff returned to his family's farm, his father, Virgil, sent word that Robert was doing poorly. Jedediah, Henry, Silas, and I brought the village doctor to see Robert. He was in a feverish state. After the doctor examined him, he told Robert and his family that gangrene had set in. His right arm had to come off right away, the doctor told them, otherwise Robert would die.

"There ain't no way in hell you're cuttin' it off!" Robert yelled.

The doctor ordered Jedediah, Henry, and me to hold Robert down while Robert's father poured a whole bottle of rotgut whiskey into him. It smelled as awful as it must have tasted. Soon Robert was properly drunk, and the doctor began his gruesome business. I almost retched as I watched the doctor cut, saw, and sew. All the while, Robert hollered like a madman. After the bloody amputation was finished, Robert fell into a feverish sleep.

During the next three months or so, Ewell's Rangers regularly rode up to Crawford's Mill to make certain that no rebels attacked any local Union farmers. From time to time we skirmished with small Confederate army patrols and drove them away.

In early March 1862, Virgil Huff made a perilous journey to Kentucky to bring letters from local farmers and villagers to family members who were serving in the Union army. He returned late that same month with letters from Union army soldiers to their relatives who lived in and around Kelley's Springs. A couple of days after he returned, he walked up to Sarah Burden and me while we stood in front of the village general store. He gave Sarah a letter from her husband, John, and gave me a letter from my brothers.

Calhoun, Kentucky
February 1, 1862

Dearest James,

It grieved us to the quick after reading what happened
to Father and Mother last Christmas Eve. We've got the
dismals mighty awful and we miss them something terrible. Thanks be to Almighty God that you're still alive.

Our officers are telling us we'll be fighting rebels
pretty soon. We've got a general goes by the name of
Ulysses S. Grant, but he dresses and looks more like
a store clerk than a general. All he's gotten us doing
is plenty of drilling, firing, and marching, and all of us
are darn sick of it all.

Plenty of us have the runs mighty bad because the
army food here is something terrible. A couple of
nights ago a cook came to our regiment and told
us we'd be eating chicken soup. He got a big pot
of water boiling on a fire, and then he took a dead
chicken, stuck it on the end of a stick, and dipped it into
the pot. After a minute or so, he pulled the chicken out
and passed out the water to us in our army cups. We
was all so mighty angry over what he done that we
beat him, kicked him in his backside, and threw him out
of our regimental camp. Sure enough, he squawked to
one of our highfalutin officers, and that officer got us to
doing plenty of extra drilling, firing, and marching. Last

night, me and Charles saw that cook making a meal
for another regiment and we told him that if he ever
came back to our regiment we'd stick him in the boiling
pot instead of the dead chicken.

There is plenty of drinking going on here. A soldier
from a Kentucky regiment invited me and Charles to his
tent where he was making demon rum. He called his
devilish drink "Kentucky head-buster" and said plenty
of soldiers in his regiment liked it. We drank a bit, and
then we drank some more, and then some more after
that. Before we knew it, we was falling down drunk.
We crawled back to our tent and fell asleep. The next
day our heads felt like they was busted and we was
throwing up and moaning a plenty. One of our officers
heard our groanings and ordered us to do guard duty
all day. We was a pitiful sight—marching back and
forth in front of our regiment's tents and throwing up
lots.

Look after yourself best you can and write us real soon.
If you're wanting to come to Kentucky and join up,
we'd be mighty happy to have you with us. Tell us real
soon what you're wanting to do with yourself.

—John & Charles

It came to be the middle of April 1862 when we heard talk
in Kelley's Springs about a terrible battle between Union and

Confederate armies at a place called Shiloh in southwestern Tennessee. Everyone told us there were many dead and wounded. I hoped—and earnestly prayed—that my brothers were safe. One evening soon after we had heard about the battle, Silas Ewell came to the livery stable where I was staying and showed me a Tennessee Unionist newspaper that listed the Union army casualties at Shiloh. He said nothing to me as I took the newspaper from his hands. I was overcome with a sense of foreboding as I read the long columns of names of Union dead, wounded, and missing. It was near the end of the lists when my eyes fell upon two names that I knew so well.

Killed—Private John Meecham (from Tennessee)
Killed—Private Charles Meecham (from Tennessee)

The worry and resentment that had stayed in my heart since that early December day when my brothers left our farmstead melted from my heart. It was now replaced with an unbearable grief and the heartbreaking realization that I was now truly all alone in this world.

Memories of my two cherished brothers have never faded. Seventy-odd years on, I can still remember the countless farm chores that my brothers and I did together, the many times we roped father's horses and rode them bareback, the cool fall mornings when we hunted for turkey and deer in Stoneman's Wood, the brotherly teasing, the wrestling matches on the front porch or in the barn, and the long, hot summer days spent fishing for catfish in the creeks near our farmstead.

9

GHOSTS

It was a Union farmer's heartbreaking story, and our own bitter memories of being driven away from our farms and livelihoods by Confederates, that galvanized Ewell's Rangers to hunt down Hiram Boldt and his rebel partisans in the spring of 1862. Nicholas Frazier, a stout and gray-whiskered farmer, had fled with his family from their farm near the small village of Sutterfield some five miles east of Hunleyville just as the planting season was beginning in April. Silas Ewell and I met him and his family at Foley's general store late that month after they had arrived in Kelley's Springs.

"They came to my place early one mornin'," Nicholas said, "and set fire to my barn and killed all my livestock."

"Did you know 'em?" I asked.

"Some of 'em," Nicholas said. "I recognized Emmett and Otis Tyrrell."

"Who was leadin' 'em?" Silas asked.

"Hiram Boldt," Nicholas said. "He helped me fix my barn a couple of summers back."

"Did you fight 'em off?" Silas asked.

"Me and my two boys, Ben and Jacob, tried, but they kept shootin' at us," Nicholas said as tears began to roll down his whiskered cheeks.

"Ben ran outside to get a better shot at 'em," Nicholas continued. "I yelled at 'im to stay inside, but he went anyway. Hiram Boldt shot him dead on our front porch."

Nicholas and his wife, Emma, wept openly, and their son, Jacob, simply bowed his head. Through his tears, Nicholas told us that Hiram Boldt and his bushwhackers had been raiding and burning other Union farmsteads east of Hunleyville.

"We heard they hanged one of my neighbors 'cause he'd stood his ground against 'em," Nicholas said, his voice shaking. "They shot all his livestock, murdered his wife, their son and their daughter, and burned their farm to the ground."

My consuming hatred of Hiram Boldt drove me ever onward as I rode with the rest of Ewell's Rangers through heavy forests and across wooded hollers one mist-filled morning in early May toward Lamont Station. The abandoned hamlet stood some three miles northeast of Sutterfield. Nicholas Frazier told us that it was common knowledge among fleeing Union farmers that Hiram Boldt's partisans oftentimes used Lamont Station as their hideout. Jedediah Woodson, Walter Tidewell, and I rode as lead scouts some ways ahead of the rest of Ewell's Rangers. Walter was riding with us because he had earned Silas's grudging trust, but I didn't swallow the story that he had undergone a sincere change of heart and had become a galvanized Yankee.

We rode along a rough country road and soon came to Lamont Station. Empty clapboard stores, an abandoned blacksmith's shop, broken wooden-planked sidewalks, and old, rusted railroad tracks welcomed us. We pulled up, dismounted, and pulled out our revolvers. We walked up and down the sidewalks, looked through dust-covered store windows, and rummaged through piles of worn-down horseshoes at the blacksmith's shop. Not a soul was seen or heard. As we tramped back to our horses, something prompted me to look back down the country road.

"Somebody's watchin' us," I whispered to Jedediah and Walter.

I pointed my revolver at a dark figure atop a horse at the far end of the road. Jedediah crossed over to the other sidewalk and the three of us strode toward the horseman. In the next instant, the horseman spun around and galloped off into the woods.

"Come on, let's get 'im!" Walter shouted.

"Don't be a fool, Tidwell," I said. "There's only three of us, and there's bound to be more of 'em in those woods."

The rest of Ewell's Rangers rode into Lamont Station. After I told Silas what had happened, he ordered my cousin Henry to take a half-dozen other rangers and ride as quickly as they could down the country road to catch any rebel raiders. Then he ordered Jedediah and me to take Walter and six other rangers and ride south through the forest for a couple of miles and then turn back onto the Lamont Station country road to trap any Confederates between us and Henry's group.

We quickly rode through mist-covered woods for several miles before we turned back onto the country road, but Hiram Boldt and his fellow rebels were nowhere to be seen or heard. We soon met up with Henry and the other rangers on the same road and returned to Lamont Station empty-handed.

"We're fightin' ghosts," I told Silas.

We spent several hours searching the woods around Lamont Station for any signs of rebels, but all our efforts were for nothing. It was well into the afternoon when Jedediah, Walter, and I reined our horses north and led Ewell's Rangers—who followed some ways behind us—through rough clearings and heavy woods back to Kelley's Springs. As we rode up to the top of a small rise in the thick woods, we heard the sound of men's voices, creaking wagon wheels, and the jangling of harnesses some distance off to our left. We turned our horses in that direction and soon reached a rough dirt road. Some yards ahead of us a wagon was being pulled by a pair of mules, and two men were sitting in the wagon seat. I thought the men might be hauling supplies for Confederate raiders or were bushwhackers themselves, so I unholstered my Colt revolver and waved at Jedediah and Henry to do likewise. The three of us then spurred our horses forward.

"Hold up there!" I yelled as we rode up to the wagon.

The wagon slowed, and then it stopped. The man holding the reins looked at us with a hard expression on his old, bewhiskered face.

"If it's supplies or money you're wantin'," the old man said, "we ain't got any. We're just poor farmers from Sutterfield."

The young man sitting beside him shifted uneasily in his seat and looked at the older man.

"I heard tell there's a bunch of farmers around Sutterfield who're Lincoln men," I said.

"Wouldn't know," the old man said. "Like I done told you, we're just poor farmers."

"What're you doin' out here in these woods?" Walter asked.

"Visitin' kinfolk," the old man muttered.

"Ain't a soul alive in these woods," I said.

"Well, they live some ways from here," the old man grumbled.

"Where?" Walter asked.

"Kelley's Springs," the young man said, his voice trembling.

"Shut your damn mouth," the old man snarled as he glared at the young man.

"What's in the wagon?" Jedediah asked.

The old man glanced at Jedediah and scowled at me.

"What're you doin' ridin' with a n——r?" he asked.

"I'll ride with whoever I damn well please," I said. "And he ain't a n——r."

"I ain't talkin' to no n——r," the old man said. With that, he turned his head and stared straight ahead.

"What's in the wagon?" Jedediah asked.

The old man cranked his head back and gave me a hard look.

"I told you I ain't talkin' to no n——r," the old man muttered.

"I reckon you'd better talk to my friend," I said. "Otherwise, he'll keep askin' till he gets an answer one way or the other from one of you fellers."

"What's in the wagon?" Jedediah asked.

The old man returned his head to stare straight ahead.

"Ain't nuthin' in the wagon," he grumbled.

"We's takin' a Yankee soldier to Kelley's Springs 'cause he's needin' a doctor!" the young man blurted out.

"I told you to shut your damn mouth!" the old man growled, and he struck the young man across the face with the back of his hand.

I reined Sugar next to the wagon and looked down into the wagon box. It was covered with a large canvas sheet. I pulled away a corner of it. A bearded man in a Union army uniform with chevrons on his sleeves lay on a small pile of hay.

"What's wrong with 'im?" I asked.

"Damn fool got himself shot in the head," the old man mumbled.

"Found 'im in our barn a day or so back," the young man said. "We tried to fix 'im up as best we could."

"You Confederates and your damn n——r can take 'im now," the old man said, "and we'll get on our way."

"We ain't rebels," Jedediah said.

The old man looked wide-eyed at Jedediah for a moment.

"Why, hell, then you black Yankees can take 'im!" the old man hollered. "It was my boy here who was wantin' to take 'im to Kelley's Springs, not me!"

I told Walter to quickly ride back to Silas and get the others. Before I could think twice, he spurred his mare and rode off into the woods. I dismounted from Sugar, grabbed my canteen from my saddle, and climbed up into the wagon box. I bent over the Union army soldier, gingerly lifted his head, and poured some water into his mouth.

"What's the soldier's name?" I asked.

"I can talk some," the soldier whispered.

He took another swig from my canteen. The left side of his head was covered in dried blood, and he was breathing poorly. After a bit of time, he began to gather some strength. As he spoke, I had to bend close to his mouth to hear his words.

"My name's Rufus Finney," the soldier whispered. "My cavalry patrol got ambushed a couple of days back. I reckon I'm the only one left alive."

He groaned and closed his eyes before his head fell back. Soon after, Walter, Silas, and the other rangers came riding up the dirt road and surrounded the wagon.

"Walter told us about this poor soul," Silas said and looked at the soldier in the wagon box.

"You damned Yankees can take 'im to Kelley's Springs," the old man muttered. "We sure as hell ain't doin' it. We're headin' back to Sutterfield."

Jedediah, Silas, and I glanced at each other. Silas unholstered his pistol, and aimed it at the old man.

"You're takin' 'im to Kelley's Springs with us, or I swear to God I'll kill you right where you is sittin'!" Silas bellowed.

"Pa, for God's sake, please, let's just go with 'em!" the young man cried out.

"I told you to keep your mouth shut!" the old man shouted.

The old man gave his son a cold, hard look, and then glowered at Silas, Jedediah, and me for a moment or two before he snapped his mules' reins and the wagon rolled forward. I stayed in the wagon box while Jedediah and Walter rode up ahead some ways and Silas held onto Sugar's reins as he and the other rangers formed two ragged columns behind the wagon and followed us back to Kelley's Springs.

It was nightfall when we came back to the village. Jedediah, Henry, and I carried Rufus Finney from the wagon into the rear room of the village doctor's office. The doctor had what I took to be a worried look on his face as he examined Rufus. After some time, he told us that the soldier's head wound was not as terrible as he'd first thought.

"It's a mighty bad wound," the doctor said, "but he'll live."

We thanked the doctor and trudged back, bone-tired and hungry, to our simple beds.

Henry, Jedediah, and I visited Rufus Finney a couple of days later. We found him in bed with white cloth bandages wrapped around his head. We introduced ourselves to him and asked him how he was faring. He told us he was faring passably.

"What happened to your patrol?" I asked.

Rufus told us his cavalry patrol was attacked by Confederates in the woods near Sutterfield some days earlier and had fought like mad demons against the rebels, but they were soon overrun. Rufus and a couple of his fellow soldiers had tried to retreat toward a wooden bridge that crossed a low-lying creek but the Confederate bushwhackers surrounded them and threatened them to give up or else.

"We knew our war was over," Rufus said in a weak voice, "so we surrendered."

The rebels pointed their carbines and pistols at them and got them off their horses, Rufus told us. They were eventually marched across a couple of empty farm fields and along a hilly dirt road that went past some farmsteads.

"A farmer came out on his porch because he must have heard all the shootin', and he yelled out, 'I see you fellers caught yourselves some Yankees! I reckon you know what you're goin' to do with 'em!' Those rebels waved at him and laughed," Rufus said, his voice growing weaker.

When Rufus and his men came to a farm, the rebel partisans ordered them to march into the barn, where they stayed for some time with no food or water. All the while, a couple of rebels guarded them from outside. However, after some time had passed, some other raiders came into the barn and ordered them outside.

"They marched us across some more farm fields and down into a wooded ravine," Rufus whispered. "Once we got to the bottom of the ravine, they pointed their pistols and muskets at us. We started beggin' 'em not to shoot us and to spare our lives, but they just kept laughin' at us."

Rufus closed his eyes. "It was murder, plain and simple," he murmured.

What I took to be a grimace of pain crossed Rufus's face.

"It was only one rebel who done all the shootin'," Rufus whispered. "A tall, skinny feller went by the name of Hiram Boldt. Had crooked teeth. I knows 'cause he kept smilin' at us while he was shootin' us."

"Hiram Boldt did the shootin'?" I asked.

"One of the other rebels hollered out as he started shootin', 'Hey, Hiram Boldt, ya like killin' Yankees?' and laughed, and Hiram just kept on smilin' and kept on shootin'. That's how come I know it was 'im that did the killin'," Rufus continued and sighed deeply.

"He shot and killed my two comrades," he whispered. "And then he came up to me and pointed his pistol at my head. The next thing I heard was a loud explosion."

Rufus told us it was only by the grace of God that he woke up sometime later lying on his back. The sky was cloudy, Rufus said, and rain was beginning to fall.

"The left side of my head was hurtin' somethin' awful," Rufus mumbled. "I felt it with my hand, and when I pulled my hand away, I saw that it was covered with blood. The buttons on my uniform had been cut off, and I had no shoes. I slowly got myself up on my hands and knees, and then I saw my two comrades lying there on the wet ground. They had no shoes on, and the buttons on their uniforms had also been cut off. I knew they was dead. It got to raining plenty hard. I crawled out of that blood-soaked ravine and across some farm fields. After a while, I got myself into a barn. I don't remember anythin' more till I woke up in a wagon and you was givin' me some water," Rufus muttered, and he looked at me.

"Who were the two soldiers with you?" I asked.

"Lieutenant Matthew Pelham was one of 'em," Rufus said. "He was a good officer. Signed up in Kentucky. Heard him tell he was from around here."

Charlotte's pretty face filled my mind for a moment and then faded away.

"John Burden was the other feller," Rufus said. "We signed up together in Kentucky. He was my best friend. He was always tellin' me about his wife Sarah, and his two boys. He told me he had a farm near abouts here."

A heavy sadness overcame me as I heard my father's cousin's name spoken. Henry and Jedediah glanced at me with deeply pained looks on their faces. We then said our goodbyes to Rufus.

While Henry and Jedediah went back to the livery stable, I walked unevenly to the dress shop at the other end of the village where Sarah Burden and her sons, Billy and Franklin, lived on the second floor. I hobbled up the side entrance stairs and knocked on the door. After a moment or two, Sarah, her face tired and careworn, opened the door and let me into the room. Worn lace curtains hung across a dirty window. Old furniture—a chest of drawers, a wooden chair, two beds, a foul-smelling chamber pot, and a small table— stood about the room. I looked at Sarah's two young sons sitting together on one of the beds. They were looking at me with large eyes set in thin, pale faces.

"Have you brought news about my John?" she asked, her voice steady and strong. "I haven't heard from him for some time."

"Is our pa comin' back?" her younger son Billy asked, his voice excited.

"Sarah, I've heard... some news about John," I said.

I told them everything that had happened to John and his ill-fated patrol. All the while, Sarah's chin quivered, but she kept looking me squarely in the eye.

"He promised me he'd come back," she whispered, her chin still trembling, "but in my heart I knew he'd never come back."

"Is there anythin' I can do for you and your boys?" I asked.

"Ain't nuthin' you can do for us now, James, exceptin' you can pray for us," she said.

"I'll try, Sarah," I said and nodded. "I promise."

I looked again at her sons. They were staring at the worn plank floor.

"It's just me and my two boys now," Sarah said. "But we'll make it through, God willin'."

Her voice sounded determined, but her chin still shook. With a heavy heart, I said my goodbyes to them as I stood outside the doorway, and I promised them I would visit as often as I could.

"Look after yourself, James," Sarah said, and she closed the door.

I stood at the threshold for a moment and heard the sounds of muffled weeping inside.

10

KENTUCKY

Through the summer of 1862, we skirmished with Hiram Boldt and his rebel raiders in the thick woods, hollers, and rough natural clearings that surrounded the long-abandoned hamlet of Lamont Station and the Confederate villages of Hunleyville and Sutterfield. My hatred of Hiram Boldt grew more intense with each clash of arms at close quarters. Once or twice, I came within a horse's length of killing him. But, at the last moment, one of his fellow rebels reined in his horse between Hiram and me, and I shot the Confederate bushwhacker dead while Hiram Boldt made a successful escape.

During this time, we also forced rebel authorities to frequently repair their local railway company's telegraph line near Hunleyville because we always cut it during our raids. Several times that summer we also rode north from Kelley's Springs to Crawford's Mill to make certain that no Confederates had it in their minds to attack local Union farmers.

Nicholas Frazier, the stout, gray-whiskered Union farmer who had fled to Kelley's Springs with his family in the spring, had given us the names of several farmers he trusted who had farms near Sutterfield and Lamont Station. All of these farmers' neighbors were loyal to the Confederate cause, Nicholas told us, but these particular farmers were Confederates in name only. Yes, they had taken the oath of allegiance to the Confederate States, Nicholas said, but taking the oath of loyalty and believing in it were two different things. In private they had told him of their strong loyalty to President Lincoln and their willingness to help the Union cause in any way they could.

"Do you trust 'em?" Silas asked.

"I trust every one of 'em," Nicholas said.

He also told us that before he and his family had fled, he and these loyal Lincoln farmers had agreed upon a secret password that Nicholas could share—along with the farmers' names and the locations of their homesteads—with any trusted Union men who needed safe hiding places or aid. Nicholas told us what the secret password was, and we used it every time we visited these rural Union sympathizers at night for help during our raids. These farmers became our Union spies. They gave us helpful information about the comings and goings of Hiram Boldt and his bushwhackers, and, as a result, we oftentimes caught them by surprise. During one particular clash in the woods near Sutterfield, one of Boldt's rebel raiders cried out, "How 'n thunder did you damned Yankees find us?" before I shot him dead.

Our spies also gave us information about local Confederate activities that we could disrupt. During one of our raids in the early days of July 1862, Walter, Henry, Jedediah, and I were given information late one night by one of our spies about a Confederate supply train that left Sutterfield every Sunday morning at six o'clock with weekly goods for delivery to several small Confederate hamlets that stood some miles southeast of Sutterfield. Our spy told us the train crossed an old wooden bridge at Snake Creek about two miles outside of Sutterfield. We rode back in the darkness to the hollow where the rest of Ewell's Rangers were hiding and told them about the train, its weekly schedule, and the bridge.

"Sunday's the day after tomorrow," I said.

"We shall fight the Lord's battle on the Sabbath," Silas said.

"Doesn't the Good Book say that every Sunday's a day of rest?" Walter asked and snickered.

"The Lord's work always needs doin'," Silas said. "Even on a Sunday."

Late the next evening five of us rangers—cousin Henry, Jedediah, I, and two others—rode across a couple of wooded hollers toward a thick stretch of woods near the bridge at Snake Creek. The single rail track from Sutterfield ran through those woods before it turned toward the bridge. We got off our horses, pulled out our axes, cut down several trees and dragged them onto the bridge and piled some rocks on top of them. We then retreated into the woods and waited for the train. Shortly after six o'clock in the morning we heard its whistle, and then we saw it: a small black steam locomotive speeding along the track pulling two boxcars and a caboose. We watched as it turned toward the bridge and in the next instant we heard the shrieking sound of steel against steel as the train engineer tried to stop the train. It was too late. The train crashed through the pile of rocks and trees and plunged into the creek, and we cheered. We got back on our horses and rode back to one of the safe farms where the rest of Ewell's Rangers were waiting for us.

It was toward the middle of September of 1862—after we had returned to Kelley's Springs from another raid—that Silas asked cousin Henry and me if we could help Virgil Huff take Rufus Finney and a local farm boy by the name of John Franklin to Kentucky. Silas told us they were planning to leave in two days' time.

"Virgil told me Rufus Finney's well enough to get back to his regiment in Kentucky," Silas said. "And John Franklin's wantin' to join the Union army."

"How long does Virgil think it'll take us?" I asked.

"Four, maybe five days," Silas said.

The next day, Henry and I went to Foley's general store to buy provisions for our journey. We gave our list of needed supplies to one of Mister Foley's store clerks, a young man by the name of Jesse Kemper.

"Hello, James," a familiar-sounding voice spoke up behind me.

I turned around. Charlotte Endicott was looking at me from beneath a faded bonnet loosely tied at her chin. Her large brown eyes were still framed by long brown curls, but her face was pale and drawn, and she was plainly dressed.

"What're you doin' here?" I asked.

"I was wondering the same," Charlotte said.

"I've got business here at the store."

"I thought you had left... I mean, after everything that happened."

"How do you know what happened?"

"I met Mister Absalom Johnson today at the livery stable. You introduced me to him at his livery stable in Hunleyville, remember?"

"Yes, I remember."

"He told me what happened to you."

"Why're you here?" Henry asked.

"I am looking for Mister Virgil Huff," she said.

"Why?" Henry asked.

"I want to go to Kentucky," Charlotte said. "Mister Johnson told me that Mister Huff goes to Kentucky from time to time."

"Why do you want to go to Kentucky?" I asked.

Charlotte told us that her betrothed, Matthew Pelham, had gone to Kentucky in March to join the Union army.

"I begged him to stay," she said. "But he told me his mind was made up."

After Matthew had reached Kentucky, Charlotte told us, he wrote her a letter, but she had only received it a month or so ago, she said, because it was difficult for Union mail to be smuggled into Tennessee.

"He told me that I should come to Kentucky," she said, "so we could get married."

Charlotte also told us that Matthew had written in the same letter that Virgil Huff from Kelley's Springs had been his trusted guide to Kentucky.

"He told me to find him," she said, "and persuade him to take me to Kentucky."

Charlotte bit her lower lip. "Can you help me find Mister Huff, James?" she asked.

"I need to tell you somethin', Charlotte," I said.

"She doesn't need to know anythin'," Henry said.

"Virgil Huff's takin' me and my cousin Henry and some other folks to Kentucky tomorrow," I said.

"I'll be damned if we take 'er with us, James," Henry muttered.

"Keep quiet, Henry," I said.

I told Charlotte to meet us at the livery stable at sunrise the next morning.

"Thank you, James," Charlotte said, smiling.

She walked out of the store. I followed her outside and caught up with her on the wooden sidewalk.

"Where are you stayin', Charlotte?" I asked.

She had found a room, she said, at the village's boarding house owned by the widow Mrs. Alexander.

"I'll see you bright and early tomorrow morning, James," she said.

"Charlotte, there's somethin' else you ought to know," I said.

I told her that a rebel bushwhacker by the name of Hiram Boldt had cold-bloodedly murdered her betrothed and my father's cousin last spring. I also told her that Rufus Finney, who was part of her betrothed's cavalry patrol and had been shot by Hiram Boldt and left for dead, was the only survivor and was going back to Kentucky with us.

"No! My Matthew can't be dead!" she cried out. "No! It can't be true!" She began to sob.

"I'm mighty sorry, Charlotte," I said.

I took her by the arm to the village boarding house and told Mrs. Alexander to take her to her room and to stay with her, and that I would visit Charlotte later that evening.

I went back to Foley's general store. Henry was at the store counter collecting our provisions from the store clerk, Jesse Kemper.

"You told 'er?" Henry asked.

I nodded.

"Have you forgotten what Judge Endicott did to me and my family?" he asked.

"I ain't forgotten."

"She's leadin' you on like a hog to the slaughter pen."

"She ain't leadin' me nowheres. I'm lettin' bygones be bygones."

Henry leaned in close to me.

"I sure as hell ain't doin' nuthin' like that," he said. "I swear to God Almighty I'll kill 'er if she gives me any reason for doin' so."

After supper at the livery stable that evening, I went to the boarding house and Mrs. Alexander led me to Charlotte's room. I knocked on the door. After a moment, the door opened and Charlotte stood before us, her face still pale and drawn, and her eyes red-rimmed. She stood aside as we stepped into the room. An old wooden wardrobe cabinet stood at one end of the room. A wooden chest of drawers with a wash basin and a rusting metal-framed single bed with a dirty cover stood at the other end. Beside the bed was a small wooden table with a kerosene lamp on it. Dingy curtains covered the room's single window. A chamber pot sat on the worn and stained wooden plank floor. Charlotte sighed deeply and sat down on the edge of the bed. I stood before her.

"Have you eaten anythin'?" I asked.

She shook her head. I told Mrs. Alexander to make something for Charlotte to eat, and Mrs. Alexander left the room.

"Are your folks lookin' for you?" I asked.

"No," she whispered.

"Why not?" I asked.

She told me that her father and mother had disowned her and driven her away from their home because she had brought shame to the Endicott family name by stubbornly staying faithful to her betrothed, Matthew Pelham, a Union man.

"And now my dear Matthew is... dead," she muttered. A sob caught in her throat as tears filled her eyes. She began to cry.

"I'm really sorry, Charlotte," I said.

She wept for a minute or two before she stopped crying and wiped away her tears.

"I don't know what to do, James," she said.

"You could stay here," I said.

"Here? In Kelley's Springs? What would I do here?"

"I'd help you find somethin' to do."

She sighed again.

"You're real decent, James," Charlotte said. "You always treated me decent."

"I reckon your Mister Pelham didn't treat you any differently," I said.

"He didn't," she said. "But after a while I learned that he loved the Union cause more than me. But that didn't make me change how I felt about him."

"He must've cared plenty about the Union," I said.

"It's the reason why he went to Kentucky," she murmured.

"Are you still wantin' to go there?" I asked.

Charlotte nodded. "I'd like to see where my dear Matthew lived... before he died," she said.

In the next moment, Mrs. Alexander walked into the room carrying a small tray of food and a pitcher of water with a tumbler. She put everything on top of the chest of drawers.

"We're startin' early tomorrow for Kentucky," I said, "so please eat and get some rest."

I said goodnight to Charlotte. I then paid Mrs. Alexander for Charlotte's room and meal and walked out of the boarding house into the cool September night.

Early on the seventeenth of September, Henry and I left our room in the livery stable and went to the stable yard. It was there that we met Virgil Huff, Rufus Finney, and a raw-boned young man by the name of John Franklin. Rufus and John thanked Virgil, Henry, and me for risking our lives by taking them to Kentucky, and I told everyone that Miss Charlotte Endicott would be coming with us.

"Endicott?" Virgil muttered. "She'll give us nuthin' but trouble."

"Send 'er back where she came from," Henry said.

"Lieutenant Pelham was always talkin' 'bout her," Rufus said. "Told me he was goin' to marry her. Does she know what happened to him?"

I nodded.

"Poor gal," Rufus said. "Well, at least she knows."

Absalom Johnson walked out of the livery stable leading a pair of tired-looking mules that were hitched to an old wagon.

"These mules ain't goin' to do you much good on those mountain trails, Virgil," Absalom said. "Best you leave 'em with a farmer I knows before you start up the trail. His name's Edward Pell."

Virgil was chomping on a small piece of chewing tobacco. He spat out some tobacco juice and nodded. Absalom told Virgil, Henry, and me the location of Edward Pell's farmstead and the secret password that would let Edward Pell know we could be trusted. We loaded up the wagon box with our provisions—dried meat, cornbread, biscuits, wooden canteens filled with water, blankets, haversacks, Bowie knives, Colt pistols, muskets, ammunition, and extra clothes. Virgil threw a small bag onto the wagon seat.

"Got letters for some of those Union army boys in Kentucky," he said.

We finished loading and Henry, Rufus, and John climbed up into the wagon box. I climbed up into the wagon seat beside Virgil who was holding the reins. He was about to snap them when I saw Charlotte hurrying toward us carrying a small bag.

"Hold up a minute, Mister Huff," I said. "She's comin'."

Charlotte hurried up to our wagon. I introduced her to Virgil, Rufus, and John Franklin.

"Still ain't sure I want 'er with us, James," Virgil muttered and spat out a thick stream of tobacco juice.

Charlotte looked at Virgil but did not say a word. She climbed up into the wagon box with help from John Franklin.

"Get up, you lazy mules!" Virgil shouted. He snapped the reins and the wagon lurched forward.

The weather favored us on the first morning of our journey and the fresh smell of pine trees hung lightly in the cool early fall air. Our wagon rattled as we traveled along the rough and hilly backcountry dirt roads that led north through thick woods toward Kentucky. It was close to high noon when Virgil halted the wagon in a small forest clearing. We climbed down and proceeded to eat our victuals while Virgil tended to the mules. After I finished eating my fare, I saw Charlotte sitting by herself underneath a large oak tree. I walked over to her.

"Are you wantin' to talk to Rufus Finney?" I asked.

"Yes, I'd like to," Charlotte said.

I went back to the wagon and returned with Rufus. After he had sat himself down beside Charlotte, I returned to the wagon.

"You reckon she's still wantin' to go to Kentucky?" Virgil asked.

"Ah, hell, just let 'er go back," Henry muttered.

"There is nothing for me to go back to, Mister Paynter," Charlotte said.

We turned. Charlotte and Rufus were standing behind us.

"But I think there is still something for me in Kentucky," she said.

We loaded the remaining food and mule feed into the wagon box. Rufus helped Charlotte climb up into the wagon box, and then he, John Franklin, and Henry climbed up into the wagon. I got up into the wagon seat beside Virgil and he snapped the mules' reins and the wagon rolled forward.

The weather stayed fair that afternoon. Oak and maple trees were starting to show their fall colors—red, yellow, gold, and orange. Looming over the woods in the near distance were a couple of low mountains. At one point as we traveled along the roads, I asked Virgil how his son, Robert, was faring.

"He ain't farin' too badly," Virgil said. "He does most of the farm chores that need doin'. It just takes him a bit longer to do 'em, seein' as how he's only got one arm to do 'em now."

Evening fell and Virgil guided the wagon and mules into a large forest clearing. He unbridled the mules, fed, and watered them, and then we ate supper. We did not light a fire because we did not want any Confederates to know we were close by. On that first night, Henry, Rufus, John, and I took turns standing watch. When it was my turn, I heard Charlotte cry out once or twice in her sleep. Early the next morning, we ate breakfast and then continued on the dirt road that would take us to Kentucky.

The second day of our journey was uneventful until we halted close to suppertime in a hidden field. Henry tramped back across it with his musket to stand watch near the edge of the dirt road. We had just begun to eat our vittles when Henry came running toward us like the devil himself was chasing him.

"Somebody's comin' down the road!" he blurted out.

Virgil, John, and Rufus gathered up our firearms and supplies and, with Charlotte in tow, hurried into the surrounding woods. I grabbed my musket and followed Henry back across the field. We hid behind some large trees and peered from behind them down the road. Four mounted horsemen with rifles slung across their backs galloped furiously past us. Hiram Boldt was leading them, with Emmett Tyrrell and two other rebel partisans riding close behind him. Henry and I watched them disappear down the road.

"How'd they know we was goin' this way?" Henry asked.

"Somebody must've told 'em," I said.

"We could've shot 'em, you know," Henry muttered.

"Are you crazy? There's four of 'em," I said, "and there's only two of us."

The image of Hiram Boldt galloping down the road stayed in my mind as Henry and I made our way back across the field to the wagon and mules. We called out to the others to come out of the woods. One by one, they came out.

"Hiram Boldt's lookin' for us," I said.

"How'd he know we was here?" Rufus asked.

"James reckons somebody must've told him," Henry said. He glared at Charlotte. She glanced at him.

"There's another road we can take at first light," Virgil said. "But it'll take us longer to get to Pell's farmhouse."

"We ain't got a choice," I said.

We ate a hasty supper and lay down to sleep. Henry, Rufus, John, and I took turns standing watch again through the second night.

We rose early the next morning and ate a spare breakfast. We traveled south for some three miles before Virgil guided the mules and wagon onto another dirt road that was harder than the one we had traveled on. The mules labored up and down the rough, uneven road almost the entire day. We stopped only once in the early afternoon to eat and drink a bit. As we traveled, Henry and I kept a lookout for any Confederate guerrillas in the surrounding woods, but the thick trees and dense undergrowth kept us from seeing no more than a few feet into the gloomy forest.

It was late that afternoon as the sun was setting when a musket fired off in the darkening woods to our right and a bullet flew past us and smashed into a nearby tree. Virgil cursed loudly and snapped the reins. The mules started pulling harder. I shouted at everyone in the wagon box to lie down, and I fired my musket in the direction of the rifle fire. In that instant, another musket erupted in the woods further up the road on our left and a bullet slammed into one of the wagon's front wheels and splintered one of its spokes.

"They're all around us!" Virgil cried out.

He snapped the reins even harder as we came to a sharp curve in the dirt road. A third musket fired from the woods directly in front of us and a bullet passed through the slouch hat I was wearing. Virgil steered the wagon and mules around the sharp turn. Henry, kneeling in the wagon box, fired off his musket into the dark woods. We traveled at a furious pace for some time through a long, narrow, and winding valley. Thick undergrowth lay on both sides of the road. Large copses of oak and hickory trees loomed in the gathering dusk.

As nightfall approached, Virgil finally halted the wagon and mules near a large grove of trees. We climbed down. While Virgil fed and watered the mules, Charlotte prepared supper for us and all the while Henry, John, Rufus, and I kept a sharp lookout for any Confederates who might be trailing us. We ate a simple supper as darkness fell, and then all the men took turns standing watch through the night.

Time slowly passed as I stood watch that night. After what seemed like an eternity, it was Henry's turn to stand watch. I made my way to where he lay asleep and shook him awake. Henry tossed off his blanket, got up, and grabbed me by the arm and the two of us went into the nearby grove of trees.

"Charlotte told Hiram where we was goin'," Henry whispered.

"Now you're really crazy," I said. "She'd never do that."

"Why don't you ask 'er?" Henry said.

I tramped back to where the others lay asleep on the ground and lay down. It was a restless night for me. We rose before the morning sun and ate a few dry biscuits for breakfast. Just as we were making ready to leave, Henry unholstered his revolver, walked up to Charlotte, and savagely grabbed her arm.

"You're goin' to tell me the truth!" Henry shouted. He pressed his Colt pistol to her head and shook her. "What did you tell Boldt and his rebels 'bout us?" he asked.

"I'm not a Confederate!" Charlotte shrieked. "I don't know what you're talking about!"

"Let her be, Henry," I said. "She ain't one of 'em."

Henry glared at me for a moment before he holstered his pistol and released his grip.

"She's one of 'em all right," Henry muttered.

"Folks," Virgil said "we'd best get movin' before the sun's up and those rebels find us."

Charlotte glowered at Henry as we put our food provisions into the wagon box. Henry and Virgil climbed up into the wagon seat and the rest of us got into the wagon box. The weather, however, was no longer in our favor, for a cold, hard, steady rain had begun to fall. Virgil snapped the reins and the mules pulled the wagon forward.

It was well past noon when we arrived at Edward Pell's homestead. Rain was still falling hard and steady as Virgil halted our wagon in front of a small wooden farmhouse at the edge of a barren farm field that was surrounded by a broken-down worm fence.

Near the farmhouse stood an old barn, and beside the barn stood a chicken coop and a hog pen. Inside the pen, a couple of hogs were rooting about in the slop. Behind the farmstead loomed a couple of low-lying mountains. Edward Pell, tall, and broad-shouldered, stood on the front porch steps cradling a long-barreled mountain rifle. We got down from the wagon and introduced ourselves to him.

"Absalom Johnson told us to stop by your place," I said, "before we got ourselves to Kentucky."

"How d'you know 'im?" Edward asked.

I stepped up onto the front porch steps, leaned in close to Edward Pell, and whispered Absalom's secret password. A toothless smile crossed Edward's creased and leathery face.

"Well, I'm mighty glad to know ya," he said. "How's ol' Absalom?"

I told him that Absalom was doing just fine. Edward proceeded to tell us that a day or so ago four riders had come up to his farmstead and asked him if he had seen anyone going to Kentucky in a wagon with a couple of mules.

"Told 'em I ain't seen a livin' soul for some time," Edward said. "Besides, I said, that trail up there ain't fit for mule or wagon."

He turned and pointed the barrel of his rifle toward a deep dark scar that ran between the two mountains.

"Did you catch their names?" Henry asked.

"Can't say I did 'cause they didn't tell me," Edward said. "And I didn't bother askin' 'em."

"What'd they look like?" I asked.

"One of 'em was tall and bony," Edward said, "and had a bunch of crooked teeth. Don't remember how the other fellers looked. All of 'em was armed, dirty, smelled somethin' awful, and were rough lookin'. They all acted mighty disagreeable, especially the tall, bony feller."

"They're nuthin' but a bunch of murderin' rebels, Mister Pell," I said.

"Is that so?" Edward said, shaking his head and grinning. "Well, I ain't goin' to fret much 'bout 'em 'cause I've got Ol' Glory with me."

He patted the long barrel of his rifle.

"We'll be leavin' these mules and the wagon with you, Mister Pell," Virgil said, "for safe keepin' till we get back from Kentucky."

"They'll be here waitin' for you when you get yourselves back," Edward said.

He walked into the farmhouse and returned some moments later with some food for us. We thanked him, unloaded the wagon, and packed Edward's foodstuffs, Virgil's small bag of letters, and what was left of our provisions into our haversacks. Virgil, John, Henry, Rufus, and I each grabbed a haversack, slung it over our shoulders, and picked up our muskets. We said our goodbyes to Edward and followed Virgil across the hardscrabble farm field. We came to the broken-down wooden split-rail fence, climbed over it, and tramped up the trail in the cold rain.

The rain fell hard and steady for the next two days and nights. We walked in the rain, ate in the rain, and slept in the rain, but no one grumbled. We made our way past rocks, broken tree branches, and thick patches of undergrowth along the trail. On the morning of the second day, we narrowly missed a rockslide. Henry made certain to keep his distance from Charlotte, but from time to time I saw him glaring at her. All the while, Charlotte kept to herself and never complained. She took Rufus's haversack from him once and carried it for a while before Rufus took it back from her. As our hard and wearisome march led us higher and higher up the trail, I looked back over my shoulder from time to time to see if Hiram Boldt and his rebels were following us. The heavy rain kept me from seeing anyone else on the trail and I hoped and prayed that it also kept us from being seen by Hiram Boldt and his men.

It was well past high noon on our third day on the trail when the rain finally stopped falling. We had been tramping along the trail since before sunrise and all of us were soaked to the bone. I was exhausted. I had slept fitfully the last two nights, wondering where Hiram Boldt and his fellow raiders were and feeling a dull pain in my somewhat shortened left leg. Soon after the rain ended, Virgil held up his hand. The rest of us halted. Virgil looked about, and then he turned to us.

"Folks," he said, "we're in Kentucky."

A smile spread across his thickly bearded face. *Hallelujah*! I thought. I looked back at the long narrow trail behind us. No one was following us.

After walking along the trail for another three miles or so, Virgil led us off into thick woods and we soon came to a backcountry road. We followed it for a while before we stopped and saw off to our right a large man-made clearing in the woods. In the middle of it stood a large wooden palisade filled with tents. A large Union flag fluttered on a tall flagpole, and smoke rose from cooking fires. Blue-coated soldiers were performing drills, riding horses, or standing picket duty. Artillery pieces with their ammunition wagons stood side by side in orderly rows. As we stood staring at the Union encampment, several Union army soldiers stepped out of the woods and approached us with muskets leveled at us. Virgil spoke some words to them and they led us to their bivouac.

11

JUDAS

Charlotte was given her own tent by the commanding officer of the Union army camp, while Henry, Virgil, and I shared a tent. On our second day in camp, Rufus Finney and John Franklin came to our tent. Rufus told us that he was leaving the next day to join another Union army cavalry regiment.

"I ain't goin' to forget what you've done for me," Rufus said.

We wished him much good luck. John Franklin stood proudly before us wearing a Union army private's uniform. Virgil, chomping on a piece of chewing tobacco, looked him over and then spat out a stream of tobacco juice.

"You look mighty fancy in that soldier's getup," he said.

"I'm also joinin' a cavalry regiment," John said, grinning, "and I heard we'll be seein' some fightin' before long."

No sooner had John spoken than a barrel-chested Union army sergeant marched up to the four of us, leaned in close to John's face, and cussed out the newly minted young cavalryman.

"Private Franklin, wipe that stupid grin off your ugly face!" the sergeant bellowed. "You ain't nuthin' but a deadbeat army private! Didn't I give you an order to clean up all the horse manure in the camp?"

"Yes, Sergeant!" John shouted.

"Why the hell's there horse manure everywhere I look?" the sergeant yelled.

John's cheeks flushed crimson.

"Get back to your post," the sergeant hollered, "and get to it!"

"Yes, Sergeant!" John shouted again and saluted him.

The four of us chuckled as John skedaddled with the sergeant right on his heels still cussing him out.

It was close to high noon on our third—and last—day in camp when Charlotte came to our tent and told us that she was leaving to work in one of the Union army hospitals in Kentucky.

"I know Matthew would have wanted me to help the Union cause," she said.

She then thanked us for bringing her safely to Kentucky. Virgil wished her good fortune. Henry said not a word to her. I told Charlotte that I would miss her.

"I will miss you, too, James," she said. "Please look after yourself."

As I watched her slowly disappear among the rows of tents, Henry walked over to me and stood beside me.

"You're still as dumb as a tree stump 'bout 'er, ain't you?" he asked.

"Maybe I am," I said, "and maybe I ain't."

Early the next morning we departed for Tennessee and arrived at farmer Edward Pell's homestead some two days later. Gray smoke rose from his farmhouse chimney as we climbed over his broken split-rail fence and trudged up to his front porch. We called out his name and Edward appeared at the door holding his mountain rifle.

"I reckoned you might be stayin' a spell longer in Kentucky," he said, "but I'm glad to see you've made it back."

He walked over to his barn and brought out our wagon and mules. We thanked him for looking after them and threw our haversacks and rifles into the wagon box. Virgil and I climbed up into the wagon seat and Henry got himself into the wagon box.

"You be sure to say hello to ol' Absalom for me," Edward said, and a toothless smile spread across his grizzled face.

"We'll do that," I said.

Edward waved to us as we said our goodbyes to him.

"Get up, mules!" Virgil cried out, and our wagon rolled forward.

We had traveled about a mile back along the same rough and hilly dirt road that we had originally followed to Pell's homestead when Henry let out a sharp cry.

"Hey!" he shouted. "Look at that!"

Virgil pulled up on the reins and we looked back over our shoulders. A tall plume of black smoke rose into the overcast October sky.

"Damn those rebels," Virgil muttered.

"They followed us to Pell's farm," I said.

"I didn't see 'em on the trail," Henry said.

"Don't mean they weren't followin' us," Virgil said.

He snapped the mules' reins and they began pulling the wagon.

"We've got to do our damnedest to keep ahead of 'em," Virgil said.

He kept snapping the reins as we rattled along the dirt road through gloomy, leafless woods. Dusk was falling as Virgil steered the wagon and mules into a small natural clearing in the forest. After we tended to the mules and ate some of our victuals, we kept a vigil through the night. It was another three worrisome days and several sleepless nights before we finally reached Kelley's Springs.

A heavy rain welcomed us home. Virgil steered us through the rain and mud to the livery stable. A pair of farmers with their mule-drawn wagons filled with fall crops passed us on their way to the village grist mill. As we climbed down from the wagon, Absalom Johnson came out of the livery stable.

"You're a sight for sore eyes," he said, smiling.

Absalom took the wagon and mules into the stable and Virgil, Henry, and I followed him on foot. Inside the stable, the smell of dry hay, worn leather, and horse manure hung heavy in the air. We took what was left of our provisions, our rifles, and our haversacks from the wagon box while Absalom unbridled the mules and led them to a stall.

We then followed Absalom upstairs. Henry and I dropped our haversacks and rifles in our room and went to Absalom's room. Virgil was already slouched in an old wooden chair and he was chewing on a piece of tobacco while Absalom sat on the edge of his rope bed.

"I reckon you've got plenty to tell me," Absalom said.

He looked at Virgil, and then he looked at Henry and me. We told him what had happened to us on the way to Kentucky, the three days we spent in the Union army camp, and Edward Pell's sad fate during our journey back to Kelley's Springs.

"God bless ol' Edward," Absalom said, his head bowed. "He was a good man."

"It seemed to me those damn rebels were always circlin' 'round us like vultures," Virgil said.

"They knew we took one of their own with us to Kentucky," Henry said.

"Charlotte ain't a rebel," I said.

"Don't matter now whether she was or she wasn't," Virgil said.

"It matters to me," Henry said.

"I told you she ain't one of 'em," I said.

"She must've told Boldt and the others 'bout our goin' to Kentucky," Henry said.

"I reckon you've things to tell us, Absalom," I said.

"It ain't me who's needin' to tell you," Absalom said. "It's Silas and Jedediah. And it ain't anythin' good. I'll get 'em over here tomorrow after breakfast."

Virgil told us he had to get back to his farmstead, said his good-byes, and left. Absalom told Henry and me that he would bring us supper and left the room. He soon came back with some food and a pot of hot coffee. After Henry and I ate and drank our fill, we trudged back to our room.

Absalom woke us late the next morning and left us breakfast and another pot of hot coffee while he went out to get Silas Ewell and Jedediah Woodson. Henry and I had just finished eating and were drinking our coffee when Absalom walked into our room, followed by Jedediah and Silas. Both Silas and Jedediah were overjoyed to see us and warmly shook hands with us.

"Thanks be to the Almighty that you've come back," Silas said.

"Absalom told us what you've been through," Jedediah said.

"We've had nuthin' but hard knocks," Silas said, "since the day after you left."

"We rode down to Lamont Station a week or so ago to give those rebels another good lickin'," Jedediah said, "and we ran into a real hornet's nest."

"They was waitin' for us," Silas said.

Silas told us they lost plenty of good Union men in that fight. When he and Jedediah and what remained of Ewell's Rangers rode over to the farms of our small group of Union spies, Silas said they found their homesteads had been burned to the ground, their live-stock had been driven away, and everyone had been shot dead or was hanging from a tree at the end of a hangman's rope.

"There ain't nobody alive now," Silas said, "who can tell us where those rebels are roostin'."

"Silas and me have reckoned," Jedidiah said, "that we've got a rebel spy among us."

"That's how they come to know 'bout your goin' to Kentucky," Silas said.

"I know who the rebel spy is," Henry said.

"Who?" Jedediah asked.

"Charlotte Endicott," Henry said.

"Ain't no way she would've betrayed us!" I hollered. "For God's sake, her betrothed was in the Union army!"

"Judge Endicott's been walkin' with the devil, James," Silas said.

"Like the Good Book says, 'a corrupt tree bringeth forth evil fruit,'" Jedediah said.

I glared at Henry, Jedediah, and Silas in turn.

"For God's sake, she ain't a Judas!" I shouted.

"I hope for our sakes that you're right, James," Silas said.

"I know I'm right!" I shouted.

"She's been leadin' you on, James," Henry said.

"That's a lie!" I cried out.

"Face the truth, James," Henry said. "She's a spy for the rebels."

"I'll never believe it," I said.

"Time'll tell us who's right," Jedediah said, "and who's wrong."

Silas told Henry and me that some of Boldt's partisans had ridden through Kelley's Springs late one night a couple of days ago and had fired off their revolvers.

"They scared plenty of folks 'round here," Jedediah said.

Silas also told us that those same bushwhackers had also tried to raid a couple of Union farmsteads some miles north of Kelley's Springs that night, but those farmers had fought them off.

"That don't mean they won't try again," he said.

The last days of September and the month of October saw no raids by Ewell's Rangers into Confederate territory. We simply sat on our haunches and licked our wounds. A Tennessee Unionist newspaper dated the twentieth of September told us of a dreadful battle that had taken place the day we had left for Kentucky. Confederate and Union armies had met in mortal combat near the western Maryland town of Sharpsburg and in a single day's fighting more than 20,000 Union and Confederate soldiers were killed, wounded, or missing in action. That same newspaper reported on the twenty-third of September that President Lincoln had issued an Emancipation Proclamation declaring that all colored peoples held as slaves in the rebel states "are, and henceforward shall be free." I told Jedidiah about President Lincoln's declaration.

"Thanks be to the Almighty," Jedediah shouted, "and President Lincoln!"

In that moment, I wondered what had become of Mister Roundtree's poor slave, Lucas.

November came and brought a harsh winter to the land. The rough weather kept Hiram Boldt and his rebel partisans from raiding Union farms around Kelley's Springs. It also gave Silas Ewell time to recruit several local farm boys to Ewell's Rangers.

Spring soon came and brought Mrs. Alexander to the livery stable on a clear and cool April morning where I was cleaning out the stalls.

"Where's Silas?" she asked.

I told her that Silas and Jedediah had gone to the widow Clay's farmstead to help with the spring planting.

"I was wantin' to tell 'im 'bout a couple of strangers," Mrs. Alexander said, "that stayed at my boardin' house last night."

.   She told me that two armed men had arrived on horseback, made their marks in her register book, and asked for supper and a room at the back of her boarding house.

"Who were they?" I asked.

"They told me they were horse buyers for the Union army," she said.

She then proceeded to tell me that after she took them to their room she went to the kitchen to make supper for them and brought it to their room.

"They was sittin' on their beds," Mrs. Alexander said, "and drinkin' the devil's water."

"Did they say anythin'?"

"I don't bother with anythin' a boarder says or does. Their business is their own. I only care that they pay for their room and meal. But one of 'em said somethin' peculiar to the other one just as I was leavin' 'em."

"What'd he say?"

"He said that Hiram Boldt would be mighty angry if he found out they was drinkin' while they was out scoutin'."

Mrs. Alexander told me that after she closed the door to their room there was a knock at the back door. When she opened it, Mister Foley's young store clerk, Jesse Kemper, stood in the doorway. She said Jesse told her he had come over to talk to the horse buyers staying at her boarding house about a horse that he wanted to sell.

"How'd he know they would be at your place?" I asked.

"Don't know," Mrs. Alexander said.

"You didn't ask 'im?"

"Ain't my business to ask questions."

"Did Jesse talk to 'em?"

"I reckon he did 'cause he stayed in their room a bit, and then he up and left."

"How do you know?"

"I see everybody who comes and goes in my boardin' house."

"Did you hear what they were talkin' 'bout?"

"I never listen at my boarders' doors."

"Are those two horse buyers still in their room?"

"They paid up early this mornin' and rode out."

"Did you see which way they went?"

"They paid me for their room and meal. They didn't pay me any-thin' extra to watch 'em ride off."

She turned and looked back over her shoulder at me.

"You'd better tell Silas," she said, and she walked out of the livery stable.

Silas and Jedediah were cleaning out the barn when I rode up to the Clay farmstead. I told them what had happened at the Alexander boarding house.

"What did that Kemper kid talk to 'em about?" Silas asked.

"Mrs. Alexander doesn't know," I said, "but I'll find out."

"Take Jedediah with you," Silas said. "And get Henry to help you."

Jedediah and I rode back to Kelley's Springs. We found Henry at the village blacksmith's shop where his mare was being shod with new horseshoes. I told Henry what had happened at the boarding house, and we left our horses at the blacksmith's shop and made our way to Foley's general store. Mister Foley told us that Jesse had just left with a wagonload of goods for Campbell's Mill. We hurried back to our mounts and rode off after him. We soon came upon him steering a one-mule wagon on a rough dirt road that ran beside Black Locust Creek.

"Hold up there, Jesse!" I hollered.

Jesse pulled up on the reins. We halted our horses in front of the wagon.

"What're you fellers wantin'?" he asked.

"I heard you were at Mrs. Alexander's boardin' house last night," I said.

"Ain't been anywheres near her place," Jesse said.

"I heard different," I said.

"She told you?" Jesse asked.

I nodded.

"She's lyin'," Jesse said.

"Ain't ever known 'er to be a liar," I said.

Jedediah dismounted, strode up to Jesse, and looked at him.

"Get the hell off that wagon, boy," Jedediah said.

Jesse gave Jedediah a cold look.

"I ain't listenin' to you, n——r," Jesse said.

Jedediah clambered up into the wagon seat, grabbed Jesse, and punched him hard in the stomach. Jesse doubled over and fell to his knees. As he gasped for air, Jedediah grabbed him by the scruff of his neck and threw him off the wagon.

"What'd you say to Hiram Boldt's men?" Jedediah asked as he pulled Jesse up onto his feet.

"I didn't say nuthin' to 'em," Jesse muttered, still gasping for air.

Henry and I got off our horses and I pulled out two coils of rope from my saddlebag. I tied Jesse's hands behind his back with one of the ropes and then made a noose with the other coil of rope, and tied it tightly around Jesse's neck.

"Get 'im over to the creek," I said.

We dragged Jesse to the bank of Black Locust Creek where I took the other end of the noose and tied it around a good-sized rock that lay on the ground nearby.

"You want to end up in there, Jesse?" I asked and pointed to the creek.

"We know you talked to those two fellers at the boardin' house last night," Henry said.

Jesse glared at us.

"You and your n——r," Jesse cried out, "ain't nuthin' but god-damned Southern traitors."

"Let's see who's the traitor," I said.

I dragged Jesse into the creek, threw the tied-off rock into the creek, and pushed Jesse's head into the dark waters.

"No!... Please!... I don't want... to die!" he spluttered, as he struggled to lift his head out of the water.

"Tell us what happened at the boardin' house!" I shouted.

I pushed his head under the creek waters again for good measure.

"Please... get me out of here! I'll... tell you! Please... get me out of here!" Jesse shrieked.

We pulled him out of the water and dragged him, wet, shivering, and sobbing, up onto the creek bank.

"Are you goin' to tell us?" Jedediah asked.

Jesse told us that he had gone to the boarding house to pass on information from his cousin, Walter Tidewell, to Hiram Boldt's men.

"What'd you tell 'em?" I asked.

"I told 'em 'bout all those fellers who joined up with your outfit last winter," Jesse said.

He also told us that it was Hiram Boldt's scheme for his cousin Walter to spy for him and his rebel partisans.

"Hiram knows my cousin," Jesse said. "He told 'im to get himself caught by you fellers, and then earn your trust so's he could spy on you."

"How do you know?" Jedediah asked.

"He got liquored up one night," Jesse said, "and told me."

"Did your cousin get you to spy for 'im?" I asked.

Jesse nodded.

"It was me who told 'im 'bout you and that girl headin' up to Kentucky," Jesse said.

"How'd you know?" I asked.

"I was workin' at Mister Foley's the day she come to the store," Jesse said. "I heard everythin' you and that girl talked 'bout in the store. And then I told my cousin and he told Hiram."

"And Hiram and his bunch tracked us all the way to Kentucky," Henry said.

"Damn 'im to hell," I said.

"What do we do with this traitor?" Jedediah asked.

I glared at Jesse as Jedediah grabbed him by the nape and shook him like a rag doll.

"Throw 'im into the creek," Henry said.

"That's the best place for 'im," Jedediah said.

I shook my head.

"No," I said. "That would be too easy. He ought to just rot in jail."

We dragged Jesse back to the wagon and took him back to Kelley's Springs.

It was the afternoon when we returned to the village. We took Jesse to the jail and the sheriff locked him up in one of the dank cells. Jedediah rode back to the livery stable with my horse and Henry's mount while Henry and I took the wagon and mule back to Mister Foley's store. We told Mister Foley what Jesse and his cousin had done and then walked over to the livery stable.

"Jedediah told me 'bout Walter and his cousin," Absalom said. "Walter's taken a horse over to Virgil Huff's place. He'll be back soon."

"We're not waitin' for 'im," I said.

We had just begun to saddle our horses when Silas rode up and I told him what Jesse and Walter had done.

"We're ridin' out to get Tidewell," I said.

"He'll get no mercy from us," Silas said.

Jedediah, Henry, Silas, and I rode out along a rough, wooded backcountry road that led to the Huff homestead. As we reached a rise in the road we saw in the near distance Walter Tidewell riding toward us. We turned our mounts into the surrounding thick woods and soon heard the sounds of a horse's hoofs on the dirt road. We spurred our mounts out onto the road and pointed our revolvers at Walter. He pulled up hard on his horse's reins.

"What're you fellers wantin'?" he asked, and a grin spread across his bewhiskered face.

"You so much as twitch, Tidewell," Silas said, "and I'll send you to hell."

Walter wiped his mouth with the back of his hand.

"Unbuckle your holster, Tidewell," Jedediah said, "and drop it on the ground."

Walter did as he was told.

"We know you're a rebel spy," I said.

"I ain't nuthin' of the kind," he said.

"That ain't what your cousin Jesse told us," Henry said.

"Jesse? That boy's a born liar," Walter said.

"He wasn't lyin' to us," Jedediah said.

"He's sittin' in a jail cell now," I said.

"And that's a whole lot better than where you're goin'," Jedediah said.

"Get off your horse, Tidewell," Henry said.

Walter hesitated for a moment and then dismounted. Henry, Jedediah, and I got off our horses and pulled out ropes from our saddlebags. We pushed Walter onto his knees, Jedediah tied Walter's hands behind his back, and I made a noose and tied it tightly around Walter's thin neck.

"Please... Please... for God's sake don't hang me!" Walter cried out. "Put me in jail with my cousin, but don't hang me!"

"We showed you mercy once, remember?" Silas said. "How'd you repay us?"

"You betrayed us," I said.

"You're a Judas!" Jedediah shouted, and he pushed Walter's head to the ground.

Walter shook like the devil had taken hold of him. Jedediah and I dragged him to a nearby large oak tree and Henry threw the loose end of the rope that was tied around Walter's neck over a thick tree branch.

"Please... For God's sake, please... don't hang me!" Walter cried out.

Jedediah and I grabbed the rope and hoisted him off the ground. While Jedediah held onto the rope, I tied the remainder of it around the base of the oak tree. Gasping and choking, Walter struggled fiercely and kept kicking his legs, but his life ended quickly. *Too damn quick for a traitor*, I thought, as we watched his lifeless body swing slowly from the oak tree.

"Praise be to the Almighty," Silas said, "for His righteous justice is done."

We grabbed the loose reins of Walter Tidewell's horse and went back to Kelley's Springs.

12

FIGHT THE DEVIL WITH FIRE

In the months that followed the hanging of the Confederate spy, Walter Tidewell, we mounted raids south of Kelley's Springs toward the rebel stronghold of Hunleyville and we gave Hiram Boldt and his Confederate raiders a good whipping every time we fought them. We also read in a Tennessee Unionist newspaper news of the defeat of a large Confederate army led by General Robert E. Lee in the first days of July 1863 by Union forces at a town called Gettysburg, in Pennsylvania, as well as the capture of the Confederate city of Vicksburg, Mississippi, on the Fourth of July by Union General Ulysses S. Grant and his army.

It was early in December when a long column of Union army cavalrymen rode into Kelley's Springs. Henry and I watched them from the livery stable as they halted in front of Foley's general store. We walked over to the cooper's shop and told Jedediah about the blue-coated cavalrymen, and the three of us walked over to the general store.

"James! Jedediah! Henry!" one of the rough-looking cavalrymen cried out.

Rufus Finney was sitting on a chestnut-colored mare and was grinning from ear to ear. We were elated to see him. He dismounted and shook hands with each of us.

"What're you doin' here, Rufus?" I asked.

Rufus told us that he and the rest of his cavalry unit were blazing a trail through the nearby woods and along several backcountry roads ahead of a large Union army advance.

"Do you know these men, Corporal?" a mounted cavalry officer asked.

"Yes, sir, Captain Wilkinson, I do," Rufus said. "They're the ones who saved my life."

The captain looked at each of us.

"And it was these two men," Rufus said, pointing at Henry and me, "who brought me to Kentucky."

"What have you folks been doing since the war started?" Captain Wilkinson asked.

"We're Union guerrillas," Jedediah said.

Captain Wilkinson shook his head.

"We don't like civilians playing soldiers," he said. "You never follow orders or the rules of war. Every time there's a battle you go off half-cocked before the fight's even had a chance to start."

I told the captain what Ewell's Rangers had done for President Lincoln and the Union cause.

"Do you trust these men, Corporal?" Captain Wilkinson asked.

"I trust 'em with my life, sir," Rufus said. "Maybe, Captain Wilkinson, since they're from around here, they could do some scoutin' for us."

"Before they do any scouting, Corporal," the captain said, "they'll have to pass muster with our commanding general, General Sherman."

Captain Wilkinson ordered the rest of the cavalrymen to remain in the village until he and Corporal Finney returned with the three of us. I walked unevenly behind Henry and Jedediah as we made our way back to the livery stable. After we told Absalom what was happening and told him to go and tell Silas the news, we saddled our horses, grabbed our firearms, and rode back to the general store. The captain led us out of Kelley's Springs.

We rode at a brisk pace in a southwesterly direction for some miles along a country road that ran past farmsteads and through forests. We knew we had arrived at a Union army encampment when a picket of Union soldiers stepped out from the surrounding woods and pointed their muskets at us. In the next moment, they saluted Captain Wilkinson, stepped aside, and waved us past. In the surrounding farm fields regiment after regiment of Union army soldiers stood at attention as Union army officers brandishing swords and revolvers paced back and forth in front of the thick ranks of blue-coated soldiers.

We rode past a long column of mounted cavalrymen and a line of artillery pieces with their ammunition wagons, artillery crews, and four-horse wagon teams before Captain Wilkinson led us off the road into a large forest clearing. We halted and dismounted in front of a picket line, to which a number of horses had already been tied.

"I've got to report to General Sherman," Captain Wilkinson said. "I'll be back."

He trudged off toward a large collection of tents that stood at the far end of the clearing.

"Well, will ya look at what the corporal's brought with 'im!" a voice cried out.

"Hey, Corporal, did you go fishin' and catch yourself some rebels?" another voice asked.

A small knot of armed Union soldiers stood near the picket line. One of the soldiers was smoking a pipe and another soldier was chewing on a plug of tobacco.

"Ain't too sure 'bout that colored feller standin' over there," the pipe-smoking soldier said. "He sure don't look like no Johnny Reb to me," and he pointed at Jedediah with the stem of his pipe.

"I reckon you'd be right, Tad," the tobacco-chewing soldier said. "He sure don't look like any rebel I've ever seen," and he spat out a thick stream of tobacco juice.

"I reckon the colored feller's workin' for 'em as a field hand on a cotton plantation," the soldier named Tad said.

As the other soldiers laughed, Jedediah took a step toward the soldier named Tad, but I pulled him back.

"These fellers ain't rebels or field hands," Rufus said. "They're Tennessee bushwhackers who're fightin' for the Union."

"Bushwhackers?" a soldier exclaimed.

"Corporal, you reckon they're 'bout as bloodthirsty as those Kansas jayhawkers we've heard plenty 'bout?" another soldier asked.

"I reckon they is," Rufus said.

"I've heard Kansas jayhawkers scalp every Confederate they kill," the soldier named Tad said.

"You Tennessee fellers scalp dead rebels?" the tobacco-chewing soldier asked.

"Every rebel we've killed so far has been bald-headed," Jedediah said.

The small group of Union soldiers glanced at each other and chuckled. In the next moment, Captain Wilkinson strode up to us.

"General Sherman is ready to see you," he said.

"Say hello to Uncle Billy for us!" Tad exclaimed.

The other soldiers snickered.

"Get back to your guard duties!" Captain Wilkinson snapped.

The knot of Union soldiers quickly untied itself.

We followed Captain Wilkinson and Corporal Rufus toward the line of tents where Union army sentries stood guard with shouldered muskets and officers walked briskly in and out of the tents.

"Why's the general called Uncle Billy?" Jedediah asked Rufus in a low voice.

"It's a nickname we've given 'im," Rufus whispered. "But don't say it in front of 'im."

I shambled behind the others as we came up to one of the large tents. A man of average height, with a close-cropped beard and short auburn hair, stood behind a wide table on which a large map lay. His general's uniform was dirty and he was chewing on a cigar stub. Standing behind him were several officers and close by a quartet of musket-bearing blue-clad Union army soldiers stood guard. Captain Wilkinson and Rufus saluted the general and he smartly returned their salutes.

"General Sherman," the captain said, "these are the Union civilians I've told you about."

General Sherman glanced at Henry and me, and then he fixed his gaze upon Jedediah. Jedediah met the general's steady look.

"You're confident, Captain, that these bushwhackers know the roads and woods that will take us to—" He looked at the map. "Kelley's Springs?" he asked.

"Yes, General," the captain said. "Corporal Finney—"

"I hope for your sake, Captain, that you're right," Sherman said.

"General Sherman," I said, "we know those roads and—"

"It's vital, Captain Wilkinson," Sherman said, "that we get to

Knoxville without delay."

"Yes, sir," the captain said.

"Some of the roads aren't even marked on this map," Sherman grumbled as he looked at the paper spread out before him.

"General, we're from Kelley's Springs," Jedediah said, "and we know—"

"My orders from General Grant are clear, Captain Wilkinson," Sherman said, still staring at his map. "The Confederate army has laid siege to our forces at Knoxville. We have been ordered to advance with all haste to relieve them."

He yanked the cigar stub from his mouth and threw it away. He swiftly pulled out another from inside his officer's blue field jacket, lit it, and began to quickly pace back and forth in front of his tent while he puffed on his cigar.

"Yes, I know, General," Captain Wilkinson said. "With your permission, sir, Corporal Finney and I—"

"If these bushwhackers of yours can guide us south of Kelley's Springs to—"

General Sherman turned, walked back to the table, and looked at his map again, "—this place called Hunleyville that's on the road to Knoxville, I can outflank from the north any Confederates who might be marching toward us from the east."

"Yes, General," the captain said.

"General Sherman," Jedediah said, "we've been—"

Sherman waved his cigar dismissively at us.

"We want you to know, General," I said, "that we've also been fightin' for the Union."

"And some of us, General, have died for the Union," Henry said.

I told General Sherman about Ewell's Rangers while he puffed on his cigar and continued pacing briskly back and forth in front of his tent. After I finished speaking, General Sherman stopped, stood stock-still, and stared at the burning tip of his cigar.

"It has just struck me, Captain Wilkinson," Sherman said, "that your bushwhackers seem to hate the enemy about as much as I do."

"We hate 'em plenty, General, sir," Jedediah said.

"Fight the devil with fire," Sherman said.

He puffed on his cigar in silence for several minutes and then he tossed it away.

"Lieutenant," Sherman said as he looked over his shoulder at one of the Union army officers standing near him.

"Yes, General," the lieutenant said.

"Write out some military passes for these bushwhackers," Sherman said.

The officer took our names and withdrew into the tent. General Sherman once again paced relentlessly back and forth while the rest of us stood and waited. Some time passed before the lieutenant came out of the tent and placed the military passes on the table. General Sherman read them carefully, signed them, and handed them over to us. Seventy years on, my Union army pass signed by Union army General William Tecumseh Sherman is among my treasured Civil War possessions and his signature is still plain enough to see.

"If any Union army soldier stops you," Sherman said, "show them your pass."

"Thank you, General," I said.

Henry and Jedediah nodded.

"All right, Captain Wilkinson," Sherman said, "take these bush-whackers of yours back where you came from. I will issue orders for my corps to follow you."

After General Sherman returned Captain Wilkinson's and Rufus's salutes, the captain led us back across the clearing to our horses. No sooner had we untied our horses' reins than a whirlwind of activity began. Union army officers hurried toward us from the direction of the tents, untied their horses' reins from the picket line, and mounted them.

"Captain," one of the mounted officers said, "we've been ordered to move on Knoxville."

Captain Wilkinson spurred his horse forward and Corporal Finney, Henry, Jedediah, and I fell in column behind him. I looked back over my shoulder. The entire mass of Union army soldiery that stretched back along rough country roads and farmers' fields began uncoiling itself like a deadly timber rattlesnake about to strike its victim.

We soon arrived back in Kelley's Springs and were followed at a distance by various Union army regiments. The Union cavalry unit that had remained behind in the village welcomed us back. Knots of curious villagers gawked at the Union regiments that followed us.

A mile or so south of the village, Kelley's Springs Road splintered into a spider's web of dead-end farm lanes and rough-hewn backcountry roads that cut through wide, thickly strewn woods that stretched for some miles in a southerly direction toward Hunleyville. The woods were gashed in places by swamps and ravines. Ewell's Rangers had sometimes followed the overgrown farm lanes to abandoned, broken-down farmhouses or weed-filled clearings to set up overnight encampments. The rough backcountry roads that snaked their way through the woods were just wide enough for two wagons to pass each other. We pulled up on our horses' reins. The Union regiments that followed us halted.

"How do we get to Hunleyville?" Captain Wilkinson asked.

"We'll follow these two roads, Captain," I said.

I pointed to a couple of nearby dirt roads.

"I'll lead some of the regiments down one of 'em, Captain," Henry said.

"And Jedediah and I'll take the rest down the other one, Captain Wilkinson," I said.

Henry spurred his horse and trotted down the nearest dirt road. Captain Wilkinson and Rufus dismounted, and the captain waved to the halted Union regiments to advance. As the first regiment came forward, Captain Wilkinson signaled it to follow Henry. Jedediah and I spurred our mounts and trotted down the other backcountry road. I looked back over my shoulder. A regiment of blue-clad Union infantrymen with shouldered muskets was following a short distance behind us.

Jedediah and I kept a constant lookout for rebels as we rode through the woods, but the thick dark trees kept us from seeing any distance inside the forest. We had just ridden up the top of a slight rise in the backcountry road on which we were traveling when a volley of musketry fire exploded from the woods off to our right. Jedediah and I hung onto the reins for dear life as our horses screamed and reared up. Almost immediately, a chorus of loud groans, screams, and curses rose behind us. We looked back and saw a terrible scene. The Union infantry regiment that had been marching immediately behind us had been hit broadside by the musket fire and a large number of that regiment's soldiers now lay in bloody heaps on the road. In the next instant, a Union colonel and several officers waving their swords and revolvers began scurrying among the regiment's broken columns.

"Regiment into the woods by the right flank!" the colonel shouted. "Regiment into the woods by the right flank!"

What was left of the shredded regiment stumbled over their fallen comrades and dashed off into the woods. Jedediah and I jumped off our horses, grabbed our rifles, and followed them. Another Union infantry regiment that had been following a short distance behind this ill-fated regiment also quickly filed off into the woods.

Inside the forest, the Union army colonel and his officers shouted orders, and the soldiers formed up into three rows. Jedediah and I took our places behind the third row. I glanced back toward the backcountry road that we had just left and saw a Union cavalry regiment gallop past, followed by several marching Union infantry regiments.

A hundred yards or so away in the gloomy woods stood several rows of Confederate army soldiers, their officers standing close by and waving their revolvers and swords. The officers wore uniforms, while the rank-and-file soldiers wore homespun civilian garb— gray or butternut-colored pants, tattered jackets, and slouch hats. A few of the soldiers wore gray-colored military kepis. Some of the Confederate soldiers were loading and firing their muskets at us, but their shots were badly aimed, for all the bullets buzzed overhead or crashed into nearby trees.

"First row, load!" the Union army colonel shouted.

The first row of Union soldiers loaded their muskets with cartridges and powder.

"First row, ready!" the colonel cried out.

The soldiers knelt on one knee with their muskets at the ready. More Confederate bullets flew overhead and snapped off tree branches.

"Aim!" the colonel yelled.

The Union soldiers raised their muskets and pointed them at the lines of Confederate soldiers.

"Fire!" the colonel shouted.

Muskets erupted. Smoke rose into the air. Through the haze, several Confederate soldiers and officers had fallen to the ground.

"First row to the rear and reload!" the colonel hollered. "Second row forward!"

The first row of Union soldiers withdrew, and the second row moved up to take their place in the firing line.

"Second row, ready!" the colonel shouted.

The soldiers knelt on one knee with their muskets at the ready.

"Aim!" the colonel bellowed.

The soldiers raised their muskets and pointed them at the Confederates. Rebel bullets still flew toward us, but now they began to hit their marks. Here and there Union soldiers fell.

"Fire!" the colonel shouted.

Muskets erupted. More gun smoke rose into the air. More Confederates fell where they stood.

"Second row to the rear and reload!" the colonel shouted. "Third row forward!"

The second row of Union soldiers withdrew. The third row of soldiers—including Jedediah and me—moved up to take their place in the firing line. My blood was heated and I felt it rushing down my arms to my hands.

"Third row, ready!" the colonel hollered.

We knelt on one knee and set our muskets at the ready.

"Aim!" the colonel shouted.

We raised our muskets and aimed them at the Confederate lines.

More Confederate bullets hit their marks among the Union ranks.

"Fire!" the colonel bellowed.

Our row of muskets erupted. Gun smoke swirled in front of us. More Confederates fell. The colonel waved his sword and revolver toward the rebels.

"All right, boys, let's at 'em!" he yelled out.

The three ragged rows of Union soldiers and officers shouted "Hurrah!" and charged through the woods toward the Confederates. I limped behind Jedediah as best I could, and we quickly found ourselves tussling with the rebels. Jedediah fell upon a young Confederate soldier, knocked his musket from his hands, and beat him about his head and face with his revolver. A Confederate officer pointed his pistol at Jedediah. I fired off my revolver and shot the officer dead. In the next moment, a rebel soldier jumped on me and knocked my revolver and musket from my hands. We rassled for a moment before we recognized each other.

"Meecham, you son of a b——h traitor! I swore I'd send you to hell if I ever fought against you!" Philip Tyrrell shouted above the din of soldiers' cries, shouts, and curses.

"It's you who's goin' to hell, Tyrrell," I shouted, my heart beating with rage, and I spat in his face.

Philip pulled out his Bowie knife, but I knocked it out of his hand. We tussled for some time before I tripped him and fell on top of him. We struggled for the knife that lay within reach, but I grabbed it first. Philip, wild-eyed and breathing heavily, gripped my knife hand, but I was the stronger one and I stabbed him in the heart. His chest heaved, and he gasped loudly. I stabbed him again, and then a third time. My hands shook and my blood was pounding in my head and ears as I pulled out the knife, wiped it on the ground, and stuck it inside my belt. I stood up and looked down at Philip. He had once been our neighbor and friend but the war had changed everything. His mouth hung wide open and his lifeless eyes stared up at the overcast December sky.

"Damn you!" I cried out, and I gave his body a savage kick.

I looked about. Scattered knots of Confederate soldiers and officers were putting up a fierce fight, but they were being overwhelmed by savage blows from the butts of Union muskets and the thrusts and jabs of Union bayonets. I saw Jedediah pointing his Colt revolver at an unarmed Confederate officer.

"I ain't surrenderin' to no goddamn n——r!" the officer yelled.

Jedediah struck the officer's face with a savage blow of his revolver, and the officer fell to his knees.

"You're damn well goin' to surrender to me!" Jedediah shouted.

Several Union soldiers grabbed the officer, roughly lifted him onto his unsteady feet, and pushed him toward the Union rear. Other Confederates threw down their muskets and raised their hands in surrender and were roughly kicked and punched by Union soldiers before they were pushed toward the rear of our advancing Union line. Other rebels turned on their heels and skedaddled away through the gloomy forest.

"You ain't nothin' but a bunch of goddamn rebel cowards!" a Union soldier hollered after the fleeing Confederates and waved his fist at them.

Another Union infantry regiment quickly marched up behind us, and the two regiments—along with me and Jedediah—chased the fleeing Confederates through the woods. Military debris—muskets, slouch hats, gray kepis, haversacks, wooden canteens, tightly rolled blankets, and cartridge boxes—marked the rebels' line of retreat.

Here and there we found exhausted Confederate soldiers lying on the ground. We pulled them to their feet and pushed them to the rear of our advancing line. As we came out of the woods, we saw in the distance ahead of us the last of the rebel soldiers running pell-mell down a dirt road toward Hunleyville. Union soldiers quickly caught up with them and those Confederates who were not struck down by bullet, bayonet, or sword threw down their arms and surrendered.

"We've whipped 'em!" Jedediah shouted.

Exhausted, but jubilant, Jedediah and I watched as the Confederate prisoners were led away.

It was a bittersweet moment for me as I walked through the village of Hunleyville. More than two years had passed since I last set foot in the village. Some of the villagers peered out of storefront windows. Others huddled in small groups along the wooden sidewalks and glared at us. Jedediah and I stopped in front of what was once the Paynter family's general store and watched as the various Union regiments made their way through the village toward Knoxville. A couple of Union infantry and cavalry regiments broke off from the blue-coated columns and took possession of the village.

Jedediah and I walked over to the grist mill and, after showing our military passes to the Union soldiers who now stood guard in front of it, wandered through the mill. The mill's pockmark-faced Confederate owner, Josiah McHenry, was nowhere to be found. We trudged over to the courthouse, showed our military passes to a trio of Union soldiers who were standing watch outside the building, and walked inside. Scattered papers and a couple of legal books were all that remained in Judge Samuel Endicott's otherwise empty office. The judge was nowhere to be found.

Jedediah and I walked out of the courthouse and made our

way back to what had been the Paynter general store where Henry, mounted on his horse, was waiting for us.

"You must've run into a hornet's nest back there," Henry said.

"We sure did," I said.

"And we whipped 'em," Jedediah said, smiling.

Jedidiah pointed to a wooden sign that hung over the store's front door. It read: "Charley Cobbs, Proprietor."

"Sure don't look like your store, Henry," he said.

Henry got off his horse and fired off a shot at the sign. A man's face briefly appeared at the storefront window and then it disappeared.

"There's a rebel inside, Henry," Jedediah said.

"I'll get rid of 'im quick enough," Henry said.

He fired off a shot through the storefront window.

"Come out of there, you rebel skunk!" Henry hollered.

After he fired off a second shot through the window, the front door opened. A man stood in the doorway holding a musket in his hands.

"Ain't enough you high-and-mighty Yankees come paradin' through here," the man said, glaring at us. "Now you're wantin' to steal everythin' in my store."

"This ain't your store, rebel," Henry said.

"The hell it ain't," the man said. "I'm Charley Cobbs, and I own this store just like the sign says."

"You're dead wrong, rebel," I said. "It belongs to my cousin here," and I pointed at Henry.

Charley Cobbs looked at me.

"Who the hell are you, Yankee?" he asked.

"James Meecham," I said.

Charley glared at Henry.

"And what's your name, Yankee?" Charley asked.

"Henry Paynter," Henry said.

"Seems I've heard talk 'bout both of you," Charley said.

"How'd you get this store, rebel?" Jedediah asked.

Charley looked at me.

"I ain't talkin' to your n———r," he said.

"Don't ever say that word," I said, "when you're talkin' 'bout me and my cousin's good friend."

"I'll say anythin' I damn well please," Charley said. "You two Yankees can go straight down to hell, and you can take your damn n———r with you."

I unholstered my Colt revolver, cocked the hammer, and aimed it at Charley Cobbs's head.

"You oughtn't to have said that, rebel," Henry said.

Charley stared wide-eyed at me as I walked up to him and pressed the barrel of my revolver firmly into his forehead.

"It's you who's goin' to hell, rebel," I said.

"My cousin means what he says, rebel," Henry said.

Charley dropped his musket and it clattered loudly on the rough wooden gallery.

"How'd you get this store, rebel?" Jedediah asked.

Charley stared wide-eyed at my revolver.

"You'd better tell us, Charley Cobbs," I said. "Otherwise, I'm goin' to blow a hole right through your Confederate head."

Charley blurted out that he had come from another part of the county to help his cousin, Sam Tyrrell, run the store.

"You rebels took my family's store," Henry said, "after you hanged my brother, and sent me and my folks to Georgia."

"I don't know nuthin' 'bout any of that business," Charley said.

"Who owned this store before the war?" I asked.

"Don't know," Charley muttered.

"It was us Paynters who owned it, rebel," Henry said.

"If you say so, Yankee," Charley said.

"Why're you so hell-bent on wantin' to fight us?" Jedediah asked.

"I ain't got no reason to fight anybody," Charley said. "I'm too old."

"But you'd still shoot a Yankee if you ever saw one," I said. "Right?"

"I just told you I'm too old to fight anyone," Charley said.

"But you wanted to fight us, didn't you, rebel?" Henry asked. "You were holdin' that musket, weren't you?"

"I was just defendin' my store," Charley said.

"It ain't your store," Henry said.

"What's goin' on here?" a voice called out.

All of us turned as a Union army officer and a half-dozen Union soldiers walked up to us.

"These bushwhackers are wantin' to kill me," Charley said.

"He's lyin'," Henry said.

"Who the devil are you?" the officer asked, looking at Henry, Jedediah, and me.

We showed him our Union army military passes.

"This is my family's store," Henry said.

"That's a lie," Charley grumbled.

"You're the one who's lyin', rebel," I said.

"I don't know who's lyin' and who isn't," the Union officer said. "Take your gripe to the Union army military court over at the courthouse."

Charley Cobbs picked up his musket and sneered at us before he turned and slammed the door shut. Henry glared at the Union officer for a moment, and then Jedediah, Henry, and I walked over to the courthouse. Henry told the Union military court the history of his family's store, only to be told that the court would look into his issue only when the war was over. Henry stormed out of the courthouse.

"Damnation!" Henry shouted. "Yankee justice ain't no better than rebel justice!"

As we traveled back to Kelley's Springs, we passed a long line of Union army supply wagons heading south toward Hunleyville. We trudged along the road for a while before we saw my horse Sugar and Jedediah's mount tethered to several tree branches at the edge of the woods. Jedidiah and I showed our military passes to a troop of mounted Union cavalry soldiers who were standing watch nearby, mounted our horses, and continued our journey in the gathering twilight. All the while, Henry kept up a near-constant complaint about Yankee justice.

We finally rode into Kelley's Springs. Absalom welcomed us back at the livery stable. Jedediah walked back to the cooper's shop while Henry and I went to our room upstairs in the livery stable and fell onto our rope beds. Henry grumbled some more about "damned Yankee justice" until sleep finally overcame us.

13

Give 'Em Hell, Boys!

General Sherman's relief of the Confederate army's siege of Union-held Knoxville, Tennessee, was followed by a hard winter. The harsh weather kept us from hunting Hiram Boldt and his mounted Confederate partisans until spring arrived. In early May, Tennessee Unionist newspapers announced that General Sherman had begun advancing with his army from Tennessee into Georgia, and the new commander-in-chief of all the Union armies, General Ulysses S. Grant, had ordered the advance of the Union army into Virginia to fight Confederate General Robert E. Lee's army.

It was also in early May when Henry and I saw four armed Union army cavalrymen ride into Kelley's Springs with a civilian in tow. They halted at Mrs. Alexander's boarding house. One of the cavalrymen, a bearded sergeant, dismounted and knocked on the front door of her establishment. After briefly talking with Mrs. Alexander, he got back up on his horse and led his fellow riders along the village road to the livery stable where Jedediah and I were working.

"Captain Wilkinson told us we'd find some Union bushwhackers around these parts," the sergeant said.

"We know the captain," I said. "And you've found a couple of Union bushwhackers."

Henry and I introduced ourselves.

"You know this feller?" the sergeant asked.

He pointed to a bewhiskered and scruffy-looking civilian who sat astride a silver-colored mare. Henry and I shook our heads.

"He rode into Hunleyville last night," the sergeant said. "Told us he knew where that rebel Hiram Boldt and his men were hidin'."

"He's lyin'," Henry said.

"I ain't lyin'," the civilian said.

"Captain Wilkinson thought you might want to talk to 'im," the sergeant said.

Henry and I walked over to the mounted civilian.

"You got a name?" Henry asked.

"George Cleggett," the civilian said.

"Where're you from, George Cleggett?" I asked.

"Me and my brother have got us a farm the other side of Sutterfield," he said.

"How do you know where Boldt's been hidin' out?" Henry asked.

"I've been ridin' with 'im since last fall," George said.

"How many rebels has he got with 'im?" I asked.

"Thirty, not countin' me," George said.

"Why'd you join up with 'im?" Henry asked.

"I hated Yankees 'bout as much as he did," George said.

"Why're you wantin' to tell us where he's hidin'?" I asked.

George told us that after columns of Yankee soldiers had marched through Sutterfield last December, some of the local Confederate farmers told Hiram Boldt they thought the war was as good as lost. Hiram had paid them no mind, George said, but a couple of days ago, those same farmers told Hiram they weren't going to give him any more supplies or shelter.

"That got his blood to a boilin' pitch," George said.

George told us that Hiram and some of his fellow rebel raiders had ridden out late yesterday and hanged a Confederate farmer by the name of Reese as a warning to the other farmers.

"How do you know they hanged this Reese feller?" Henry asked.

"I was with 'em when they hanged 'im," George said. He shook his head. "I told Hiram I didn't join up to ride 'round hangin' Confederates."

"What'd he say?" I asked.

"He told me if I wasn't with 'im, then I was against 'im," George said.

"How'd you get to Hunleyville?" Henry asked.

"After Hiram done said his piece," George said, "I reckoned I'd better skedaddle before they threw a noose 'round my neck."

George said that as they rode back to their hideout as night was falling, he spurred his horse and rode off into the woods. Revolver shots followed after him, he told us, but he got away in the dark and hid out in the forest.

"It was late last night when I got to Hunleyville," he said. "I told the first Yankee soldier I saw that I had somethin' mighty important to tell his commandin' officer."

"You reckon Hiram Boldt's still in his hideout?" I asked.

George shrugged. "Maybe he is," he said. "And maybe he ain't."

"Henry, get Jedediah and tell 'im what's happened," I said. "I'll find Silas and we'll get the rest of our bunch here quick as we can."

It was high noon when Henry and I, along with Jedediah, Silas, and fifteen other farmers and villagers who now formed Ewell's Rangers, gathered at the livery stable. The sergeant and his fellow cavalrymen then led us with George Cleggett in tow at a furious gallop to Hunleyville, and we soon arrived in the village. Most of the villagers stayed in their stores or homes, but a few ventured outside, only to be driven back into their domiciles by Union soldiers who stood guard at various places in the village.

The sergeant led us to the gunsmith's shop where we dismounted. The Union soldiers who stood guard outside allowed the sergeant, Silas, Henry, Jedediah, George Cleggett, and me into the store. Captain Wilkinson was sitting behind a desk as we walked into the store and stood up as we approached him. After he returned the sergeant's salute, I introduced Captain Wilkinson to Silas.

"We need your help, Captain," Silas said. "We've got a chance to whip Boldt and his men but good this time."

"How many men have you got?" the captain asked.

"Countin' myself, there's nineteen of us," Silas said. "Cleggett's told us that Boldt's got thirty of his bunch."

The captain thought for a moment.

"I've only got a small number of cavalry in reserve," the captain said, "and the rest of my men are guarding the village."

"If you could spare us any aid, Captain," Silas said, "I'd consider it a blessin' from the Almighty."

The captain shook his head. "Sorry, Mister Ewell," the captain said. "I wish I could help you, but I can't. I can only wish you good luck."

Silas turned to Henry, Jedediah, and me.

"Well, boys," Silas said, "looks like we've got to help ourselves in findin' Boldt and his men before they skedaddle."

George Cleggett told us before we left Hunleyville that Boldt's hideout was hidden in thick and swampy woods some two miles south of Sutterfield. The village itself stood some five miles east of Hunleyville. Our column—George Cleggett and Henry in the lead—galloped along a rough, thickly wooded backcountry road that ran in a southeasterly direction and skirted Sutterfield from the south. Shortly after we rode past Sutterfield, George Cleggett reined his horse off the road and led Henry and the rest of us onto a narrow trail that cut through the heavy woods.

We formed up in a single file, unholstered our revolvers or pulled out our carbines, and guided our horses along the trail as it descended into a heavily wooded holler. All was deathly silent except for the jangling of horses' bridles, the creaking of leather saddles, and the occasional snapping of small tree branches as we made our way through the dark forest. Logs were laid across patches of swampy ground, and we guided our mounts across them. We soon found ourselves in a wide clearing.

"This is where Boldt's been hidin' out," George said.

Thin wisps of woodsmoke curled upward from several fire pits. A few torn and dirty blankets lay scattered on the rough ground.

"Where's he at?" Henry asked.

"Maybe he heard us comin' and rode off," Jedediah said.

"We've come too late," Silas said, shaking his head.

We sat on our mounts and looked about us. I looked at George Cleggett.

"Is this trail the only way in and out of here?" I asked.

George shook his head.

"Hiram ain't thick-headed enough to be pickin' himself a hidin' place that's got only one way of comin' or goin'," he said.

"There's another way out of here?" Henry asked.

"Over there," George said.

He pointed toward the far side of the clearing where an over-grown trail cut through the heavy woods. We formed up in a single file and, with George and Henry again in the lead, we rode across the clearing and guided our mounts along the rough, winding trail. The sound of snapping tree branches, the creaking of leather saddles, and the jangling of horses' bridles echoed once again through the eerily silent woods.

It took us some time before we finally rode out of the woods and onto an abandoned farm field that was surrounded by thick forest on three sides.

"We'll fight that devil Hiram Boldt and his demons in the Valley of Elah," Silas hollered. "Almighty God shall be our strength! There shall be no mercy for the wicked!"

In the next instant, we heard the loud *crack!* of a musket shot and George Cleggett fell sideways off his horse. We pulled up on our horses' reins as Hiram Boldt and his mounted rebel raiders burst into the farm field from the surrounding woods.

"Give 'em hell, boys!" Silas cried out.

We fired off our revolvers and carbines and our shots knocked more than a few rebel partisans out of their saddles. The charging rebels replied with a fusillade of their own and a number of our men fell from their mounts. Two Confederates subsequently charged at me, hollering foul oaths, but I shot them both dead with my Colt. I saw a rebel trying to get back onto his horse after he had fallen off and I shot him dead too. A mounted Confederate tried to pull me off Sugar, but I struck him across the face with the barrel of my revolver and shot him and he fell backward off his horse.

Carbines and pistols fired off in every direction. Bullets flew like hornets bursting out of a hornet's nest. Thin clouds of gun smoke filled the air. The melee became wild and furious as Yankees and Confederates cursed and hollered at each other, shot at each other, and pulled each other off their horses. Fearsome hand-to-hand clashes broke out as dismounted Yankees and Confederates tussled and stabbed each other with Bowie knives, choked each other, and tried to gouge each other's eyes out. Riderless horses screamed and galloped wild-eyed across the farm field and broke through the thick walls of trees.

I saw a small group of dismounted rebels forming a firing line, and I waved at Jedediah and several other rangers to follow me. We charged them and they broke and skedaddled as fast as their legs could carry them. We chased them down and shot them all dead.

The vicious and bitter fighting soon came to an end. In its wake there rose loud groans and mournful cries for aid and water. Horses lay dead or mortally wounded. Bodies—Yankee and Confederate— lay where they had been wounded or killed in mortal combat. Jedediah and I dismounted from our horses and walked among the dead, dying, and wounded.

"Where's Hiram Boldt?" I asked.

"Don't see 'im," Jedediah said.

Soon enough we found Silas lying on his back, his jacket blood-soaked. He was trying to pull out a small Bible from his jacket pocket. He had once told me that his long-departed mother had given it to him when he was a boy. Jedediah and I knelt beside him. We grasped Silas's hands, and I bent my ear close to him.

"I've fought the good fight, James," Silas murmured. "I've fin-ished my course, and I've kept the faith."

He then let out a long slow breath and died. I slowly folded Silas's arms across his chest, closed his eyes, and took his blood-stained Bible from his jacket pocket. Jedediah rose and walked over to several bodies that lay nearby.

"I've found Henry," he said.

Henry lay face down on the ground, his Colt revolver still in his hand. His slouch hat lay on the ground beside him. I kneeled on the ground and turned him over. His head was covered in blood and dirt, and he had mercifully gone to glory. Tears gathered in my eyes and rolled down my unshaven cheeks as I prayed over Henry. In the meantime, Jedediah had wandered over to the edge of the woods and come running back.

"Emmett Tyrrell's over by those trees," he said pointing to the nearby woods.

I followed Jedediah into the forest. Emmett, hatless, was slowly crawling on his hands and knees among the trees and bushes. I kicked him, and Emmett, bleeding from several gunshot and knife wounds, fell onto his back with a loud cry.

"Where's Hiram Boldt?" I asked.

He glared at me.

"You'll never get 'im, Meecham," he muttered. "Dead, or alive."

I unholstered my Colt revolver.

"It was Hiram, and you, and your brother Otis," I muttered, "who killed my folks."

"I swear to you, Meecham," he said, gasping, "it wasn't me that killed 'em."

"You're lyin'."

"I swear to God I ain't lyin'."

I pointed my revolver at his head. "You're a liar."

"Please... for God's sake, don't kill me!" Emmett cried out, his voice shaking.

I cocked the hammer.

"Please, don't! I've got myself a wife, and a little—"

I pulled the trigger.

Night fell. We lit small fires around the farm field and buried the dead where they had fallen. We treated the wounded as best we could.

It was past noon the following day when we rode away with the wounded—Union and Confederate—in tow. Exhausted and half-asleep, I almost fell out of my saddle, but Jedediah caught me by the arm at the last moment.

It was some time before our weary and ragged column reached Kelley's Springs. Soon enough, the village doctor was busy cutting flesh, sawing bones, and sewing up the stumps of arms and legs. While the doctor went about his dreadful business, I rode over to the Ewell homestead. I said my hellos to Silas Ewell's kinfolk. With a heart filled with great sorrow, I told them that Silas had died for a righteous cause and had always shown a fatherly care for me. His widow wept and his other relations looked on with sad looks upon their faces as I gave his widow Silas's small blood-stained Bible. I said my goodbyes and made my way back to Kelley's Springs.

14

JUDGMENT DAY

By the late summer of 1864, the Union army had established large and well-armed garrisons across our part of the county. Union army cavalry patrols were now a regular sight. Rumors soon abounded that many Confederate farmers in our part of the county were taking oaths of allegiance to the Union and betraying what remained of Hiram Boldt's mounted rebel raiders. Singly or in small groups, these rebel bushwhackers were captured by the Union army and brought to Kelley's Springs. They were a pitiful sight to see—thin, starving, shabbily clothed, filthy, and, in many cases, badly shod. Several of Boldt's raiders, however, including Hiram Boldt himself, still remained at large as the fall harvest season drew near.

It was early September when two Union army cavalrymen rode into Kelley's Springs and found me in the livery stable.

"We caught one of Boldt's men yesterday," one of the cavalrymen said. "He's in the Hunleyville courthouse jail."

"Does he have a name?" I asked.

"Says he's Otis Tyrrell," the other cavalryman said. "Says he wants to talk to you."

Jedediah and I rode back with the two cavalrymen to the village of Hunleyville. Otis Tyrrell—ragged, filthy, and foul-smelling—was sitting on a rope bed in one of the courthouse's dank cells.

"Why're you wantin' to talk to me?" I asked.

Otis reached into his soiled jacket, pulled out a plug of tobacco, took a bite, and began chewing.

"These Yankees are goin' to hang me in a couple of days," he said.

"What the hell d'you expect?" I said. "You're a rebel bushwhacker, ain't you?"

"If I was you," Jedediah said, "I'd be on my knees prayin' to the Almighty to save my soul."

Otis spat out a thick stream of tobacco juice and his snake-like eyes settled on Jedediah.

"Ain't ever had a mind for religion or for prayin'," Otis muttered.

He then shifted uneasily on the rope bed, and his reptilian eyes settled on me.

"Hiram's told me plenty 'bout you, Meecham," he said. "And I knows plenty 'bout 'im."

"What d'you know 'bout Hiram," I said, "that I don't already know?"

"Pity 'bout your folks, Meecham. I mean, dyin' the way they done."

"You ought to know. You and your brother murdered 'em."

"It weren't me and Emmett that done it. But we seen who done it."

"Who killed 'em?"

"Hiram."

"Hiram?"

Otis nodded. "And that ain't all he done that night."

"What else did he do?"

Otis looked away.

"What else did he do?" I asked.

Otis looked at his threadbare shoes.

"He... tried to force himself on your mother, but she fought 'im off like a demon, so he beat her face with the barrel of his Colt. And then that son of a b——h kept shootin' 'er till I finally told 'im to stop."

His words hit me like a blacksmith's hammer blow and a sharp splinter of pain pierced my heart. In that moment, I recalled in my mind all the dreadful sights, sounds, and smells of that horrible night—the family farmstead in flames, the livestock on fire, and the bodies of my murdered father and mother.

"It weren't right what he done," Otis said. "It just weren't right," and he spat out another stream of tobacco juice.

I felt Jedediah's hand on my shoulder.

"I'll make you a deal, Meecham," Otis said. "Save me from getting' hanged and I'll give you Hiram Boldt."

I looked at Jedediah. He was glaring at Otis.

"His neck for mine, Meecham," Otis said. "Sounds like a fair trade to me."

"If you're foolin' us, Otis Tyrrell," Jedediah said, "I swear to God I'll hang you myself."

"Are you goin' to let your n——r talk that way to me, Meecham?" Otis asked.

"He ain't a n——r," I said. "And he can talk to you any damn way he likes."

Otis grunted and shook his head.

"You remember Walter Tidewell, James?" Jedediah asked.

"I remember that rebel traitor," I said. "We hanged 'im 'cause he betrayed us."

"You hear that, Otis Tyrrell?" Jedediah asked.

"I ain't deaf, n——r," Otis said. "Have we got us a deal or not, Meecham?"

"Tell me where Boldt is," I said.

Otis shook his head and spat out yet another stream of tobacco juice.

"Your word, Meecham, that those goddamn Yankees won't hang me," he said, "and then I'll tell you."

I shook my head.

"You tell us where Hiram's at," I said, "and then I'll decide if you're fit for hangin'."

Otis sighed and shifted uneasily on the rope bed again.

"Let me tell you a story, Meecham," he said. "Me and Hiram, we was headin' toward Birch Tree Creek. That's some ways east of Sutterfield. It's got a shallow crossin' called Thompson's Ford. There's a back road called Thompson's Pike right by that crossin' that'll take you right on to Kentucky. Hiram said that as soon as we got across that ford, we'd meet up with a Confederate farmer by the name of Isaiah Porter who'd take us to Kentucky. Well, we was all worn out from all the ridin' we'd done that day, so we rested up a bit in a holler just the other side of Sutterfield. Well, damned if some Yankee cavalrymen didn't find us and got to shootin' at us."

Otis told us that Hiram told him to hold off the Yankee cavalrymen until he got clear of the holler and then to follow him.

"Hiram skedaddled," Otis said, "and I held 'em off as long as I could. But I got shot in the leg, and then my horse got shot, and... well... here I is sittin' in this goddamn jail cell."

"Hiram didn't come back for you?" I asked.

Otis shook his head. "He ain't ever cared for nobody but himself," Otis said. "Always goin' on 'bout how he had more guts and brains than any Confederate army general. To my way of thinkin', he sure weren't no Robert E. Lee or Nathan Bedford Forrest."

"When're you supposed to meet this Isaiah Porter?" I asked.

"Day after tomorrow," Otis said. "At Thompson's Ford at high noon."

A pained look crossed his dirty face.

"Damnation!" he said. "This leg hurts me somethin' fierce."

"Why the hell don't you get a surgeon to fix it?" I asked.

"I ain't wantin' no sawbones cuttin' off my leg," Otis said.

"What're you grumblin' about, Otis?" Jedediah said. "After the doctor's fixed you up, you'll still have one good leg to stand on so's you can dance with the ladies," and he cackled.

Otis glared at Jedediah and spat out another stream of tobacco juice.

"I've done told you where you can get 'im," Otis said. "Now give me your word, Meecham, that I ain't goin' to be hanged by any Yankees."

Jedediah and I walked away from Otis's cell.

"Give me your word, Meecham!" Otis called out. "Dammit, Meecham! Give me your word!"

Jedediah and I made our way to the courthouse. I spoke to a Union army officer and then we rode back to Kelley's Springs.

Near high noon two days later, in a heavy rain, Jedediah and I—along with six other members of Ewell's Rangers—ambushed the Confederate farmer Isaiah Porter on Thompson's Pike. We persuaded him to tell us that, yes, he was meeting Hiram Boldt and his rebel companion at noon that day at Thompson's Ford, and, yes, he was taking them to Kentucky.

"You're sure 'bout that?" I asked.

Isaiah nodded and told us that he was never surer about anything in his whole life. We guided our horses into thick, wet leafy woods near Thompson's Ford. I looked at Jedediah and the other rangers as they formed up in a ragged line beside me. We were a weary-looking bunch. Lean and sharp-faced, we slouched in our worn leather saddles, our boots and long coats and horses were splattered with mud, our rough collars were turned up, and our hats and coats were dripping wet from the pouring rain. I was exhausted. My stomach grumbled, my teeth chattered, I was soaked to the bone, and my left leg and back hurt something awful. My horse Sugar snorted and shook her head, and her bridle jangled.

"You're sure he's comin' this way?" Jedediah asked.

"That's what Otis told us," I said.

"I don't trust 'im," Jedediah said.

"He knows we'll hang 'im if he's lied to us," I said.

"What about our rebel farmer?" Jedediah asked.

We glanced back over our shoulders at Isaiah Porter. He was sitting on his mare with his hands tied behind his back and one of our rangers was pointing his Colt revolver at him.

"He knows what's goin' to happen to 'im if he's lied to us," I said.

"We should've left Boldt alone, like I told you," Jedediah grumbled. "What can he do now that this war's almost over?"

"I want 'im for myself," I said. "Dead, or alive."

I peered through the dripping woods. A horse and rider were slowly making their way across Thompson's Ford.

"He's comin'," I said.

Jedediah signaled to the others. The ranger watching Isaiah

Porter grabbed the reins of Isaiah's horse and led him deeper into the woods. The rest of us pulled out our carbines or unholstered our revolvers.

"Wait till he gets to the road," I said.

Jedediah nodded.

Hiram Boldt and his mount reached the near side of the crossing. He came up out of the creek waters and spurred his horse up onto Thompson's Pike.

"Get 'im!" I shouted.

We spurred our horses, burst out of the woods, and surrounded Hiram. A look of what I took to be shock crossed his gaunt, bearded face, and then he glared at us.

"The war's over, Hiram," I said.

"No, by thunder, it ain't over!" Hiram shouted.

"It's over, Hiram," Jedediah said.

"There's others comin'."

"There ain't no others comin'," I said.

"You're a damn liar, Meecham! I know there's others comin'!"

I shook my head.

Hiram looked at each of the faces glaring at him.

"Why'd you kill my folks, Hiram?" I asked.

"Why? They was fightin' on the wrong side."

"Why did you... I mean... you tried... my mother."

A grin spread across Hiram's face.

"Why? It's 'cause I wanted to," he said.

I fired off my Colt. Hiram's grin remained frozen on his face. I cocked the hammer again and fired a second time. Hiram fell off his horse. I dismounted from Sugar and walked over to where Hiram was lying on the ground.

"I should've let you drown that day at Mule Shoe Creek," Hiram muttered and glared at me.

I cocked the hammer again on my Colt.

"You ain't nuthin' but a goddamn cripple," Hiram murmured.

I pointed my Colt at his head.

"I'll see you in hell, Meecham!" Hiram croaked.

The long-simmering blood vengeance that I had sworn against Hiram Boldt boiled over into a white-hot spasm of rage and I pulled the trigger.

We threw Hiram's body over his horse's saddle and brought him and Isaiah Porter to Hunleyville. A Union army guard detail locked up Isaiah in one of the cells and dragged Otis Tyrrell out into the pouring rain to help identify Hiram's mortal remains. A small knot of Union army officers stood close by.

"That's 'im," Otis said.

"Otis Tyrrell," one of the officers said, "your sentence of death by hanging has been suspended."

Otis looked at me.

"They ain't goin' to hang you, Otis," I said.

As the guards dragged Otis back to his jailhouse cell, he looked over his shoulder.

"You kept your word, Meecham," he called out.

Jedidah and I watched as two Union army soldiers took hold of the reins of Hiram's horse and led it toward the village cemetery.

"We should've hung 'em both," Jedediah said.

"This land's been soaked in enough blood," I said.

We got up on our mounts and rode back through the mud and rain to Kelley's Springs.

"Look at the sight of you!" Mrs. Alexander snapped. "You're a mess! And you both smell like you've been rollin' 'round in a hog pen!"

She stood in the hallway of her boarding house, her hands on her broad hips and a look of stern matronly disapproval on her face. Jedediah and I—dripping wet, hungry, and mud-splattered—stood shamefacedly before her.

"I keep a clean and tidy rooming house," she said. "So, you ain't goin' to be sittin' on my furniture or eatin' off my good plates till you've had a good scrubbin'!"

Jedediah and I glanced at each other.

"You know my usual rate for a meal, bath, and laundry," she said. "Pay up!"

Jedediah reached into his jacket pocket, pulled out some coins, and dropped them into her outstretched hand. She counted them out carefully, then waved at Jedediah to follow her down the hallway to the bathing room.

The boarding house turned quiet save for the *tick-tock* sound of a tall grandfather clock that stood in the hallway. I peered inside the parlor room. Horsehair chairs and couches. Small wooden side tables. A roll-top desk. Faded area carpets on the parlor's wooden floor. Yes, indeed, Mrs. Alexander kept a clean and tidy rooming house. I stepped out onto the wooden front porch and into the cool evening air. Out of the spreading darkness a mounted rider hurriedly rode past.

"Hurrah!" he cried out. "General Sherman's taken Atlanta! Atlanta's ours! Hurrah for General Sherman!"

I unbuckled my gun belt and stepped back inside Mrs. Alexander's boarding house.

15

ENDINGS

The American Civil War carried on for some six months after the capture of the city of Atlanta, Georgia, by Union army General William T. Sherman and his soldiers. For Ewell's Rangers, however, our war against Confederate bushwhackers ended on that muddy and rain-filled September day when I shot Hiram Boldt dead.

In April 1865, Tennessee Unionist newspapers reported in bold headlines that Confederate General Robert E. Lee had signed the terms of surrender offered by Union General Ulysses S. Grant at Appomattox Courthouse in Virginia. After four long years of bloodshed, misery, and suffering, the American Civil War had come to an end.

For a period of time, after the war ended, I stayed in eastern Tennessee and hired myself out as a laborer. Absalom Johnson died soon after the end of the war. Jedediah Woodson moved to Mississippi to be close to his relatives, and we kept up a regular written correspondence until he died in 1927.

I worked on farms and in various general stores but soon grew tired of that life and made my way to the Arizona Territory to make my fortune. I worked as a miner in several silver and gold mines, and, for a time, I was also a deputy marshal in several towns across that territory. It was as a deputy marshal that I crossed paths with several outlaws and gunslingers, as well as more than a few hardened Confederate army veterans still wearing butternut or gray who drifted through the territory seeking to make their own fortunes.

In the mid-1890s, I headed north to Kansas and came to the hardscrabble town of Blunt where I settled there as a farmer, and, later, became a town merchant. I have remained in that town to this day.

I am ninety years old now and suffer from a few of the ailments that come with old age, but I put my hand to the plow and wrote these reminiscences of my youth during the American Civil War. I have no living kin who could receive this memoir of mine once I have gone to glory, so I will leave it in the hands of the town librarian with the earnest hope that someone will come to the library one day and read my story.

Memories of my boyhood and youth in eastern Tennessee fill my mind in the winter of my life. The people I once knew and loved—Father and Mother, my brothers John and Charles, my cousins David and Henry and their parents, Father's cousin Robert Burden and his wife Sarah and their two sons Franklin and Billy, dear Charlotte, Jedediah, Absalom, and Silas Ewell—visit me frequently in my dreams before they too soon depart from me to wander across this leavened land.

James Meecham
Blunt, Kansas
July 4, 1934

THE END

Author's Afterword

Except for Union army Generals William T. Sherman and Ulysses S. Grant, all the characters, settings, and events in this historical novel are the product of my imagination.

The American Civil War ended 160 years ago, but the echoes from that long-ago war still reverberate in today's America. As William Faulkner, the Nobel Prize-winning American writer, once put it, "The past is never dead. It's not even past."

The American Civil War began on April 12, 1861, with the capture by Confederate forces of the federal-held Fort Sumter in Charleston, South Carolina. In June 1861, Tennessee became the last state to secede from the Union following a referendum in which a majority of Tennesseans voted to join the Confederate States of America. In eastern Tennessee, however, citizens voted against secession by more than two to one (33,000 votes to 14,000 votes), leaving that region's population divided between those who remained loyal to the Union and those who swore allegiance to the Confederacy. In this divided part of Tennessee, Union and Confederate bushwhackers fought each other in deadly skirmishes and carried out reprisals on the civilian population.

During my research for my historical novel, I consulted the following historical sources: the East Tennessee Historical Society website and its digitized selection of letters, diaries, and journal entries written by eastern Tennesseans (Union and Confederate) during the Civil War; a diary written by Eliza Rhea Anderson Fain, an east Tennessean Confederate, titled *Sanctified Trial* (edited by John N. Fain, University of Tennessee Press, 2004); *War at Every Door: Partisan Politics and Guerrilla Violence in East Tennessee, 1860-1869*, by Noel C. Fisher (The University of North Carolina Press, 1997); and *Mountain Rebels: East Tennessee Confederates and the Civil War 1860-1870*, by W. Todd Groce (The University of Tennessee Press, 2000).

Thomas Mauser

ACKNOWLEDGEMENTS

I want to express my heartfelt gratitude to my late aunt, Mimi (Marija) Mauser, from Cleveland, Ohio, who sparked my life-long interest in the American Civil War when she gave me a copy of Robert E. Alter's book, "Heroes in Blue and Gray," when I was ten years old. Without her generous gift all those years ago, this novel would never have seen the light of day.

Writing, it is said, is a solitary pursuit. Yet, every writer – beginner or seasoned – needs a community of like-minded writers who offer support, friendship, and constructive feedback at every stage of a writer's work. In this regard, I was fortunate to be a part of the Historical Fiction Writers Group (HFWG) in Toronto, Ontario, Canada, for nearly six years, during which time I received much helpful and critical feedback concerning my American Civil War novel from a wonderful community of historical fiction writers. In particular, I want to express my gratitude and thanks to Frann Harris, Cynthia Malik, Mark MacDonald, Gilbert Reid, Richard Willis, and the late Joan Roberts for their friendship, untiring encouragement, and unfailing patience in reading the various rough drafts of my story. My sincere hope is that the novel I have finally written will meet with their approval.

A writer always needs an excellent editor, and in this regard I was richly blessed in working with David Aretha (Book Editing Services - davidaretha.com), an award-winning author and editor, whose critical eye, sound judgment, and common sense advice helped me successfully navigate my way through the various editing revisions of my novel.

Beta readers play an important role in the latter stages of a writer's work, and I was blessed with receiving extremely positive, constructive, and helpful feedback from Lydia Pilot (fairytalesandtea.com), Bill McCreadie, James Foronda, and Starr Baumann (Quiethouse Editing - quiethouseediting.com).

My publisher, Munn Avenue Press, has been unfailingly supportive and enthusiastic as they brought my Civil War novel to life. In particular, I want to express my heartfelt appreciation and thanks to Charles Levin, founder and President of Munn Avenue Press, Lily Drew, Neil Szigethy, and Celina De Leon for their encouragement, dedication, and support throughout this entire process.

Finally, this novel is dedicated to my beautiful wife, Adriana. Her never-ending love, support, and encouragement has truly been a blessing to me.

About the Author

Thomas Mauser has been interested in history and especially the American Civil War since he was ten years old. He held various technical and management roles in his nearly forty-year career in the Information Technology (IT) industry in Canada before successfully transitioning to a second career as an English language teacher and tutor.

Now retired, he is pursuing his passion for writing historical fiction. A former member of the Historical Fiction Writers Group (HFWG) in Toronto, Ontario, Canada, Thomas now spends his time visiting Civil War battlefields, travelling with his wife Adriana to Italy, England, Slovenia, and the United States, enjoying the great outdoors, reading historical fiction, and working on his next historical novel. A cancer survivor, Thomas strongly believes that life should be lived with faith and perseverance.